WHO'S YOUR DADDY?

A Novel By

CRAIG SEYMOUR

For Morgan

"What are we to one another?"

– Andrew Holleran

Part One

Chapter 1

"I can't believe you're breaking up with me," Michael said, his head in his hands.

"I just think we want different things, like we're in different places," said Jimmy. He sat next to Michael on a queen bed tucked into the corner of Michael's bedroom.

"Different places? What do you mean different places?" Michael asked, his voice rising to a pre-pubescent squeak. "I thought we had fun together."

"We do," said Jimmy, scooting off the bed. "We did. But there's more to life than having fun."

"I don't understand," said Michael. He looked at Jimmy standing naked in front of him. Jimmy's dick—still a little red from recent activities—dangled in a tuft of reddish blond curls.

"All you ever want to do is go out and get drunk with your friends," said Jimmy, bending over to pick up his Fruit of the Loom boxers from the floor. "It's a pain to even get you to stay in and watch a movie."

"We watched *Love, Actually* last Saturday." Michael said.

"Yeah, but you kept trying to get me to blow you through the whole film," Jimmy said. He grabbed his khakis from the back of a metal folding chair.

"You know British accents make me horny," Michael whined.

"That's not the point," Jimmy said, pulling on his pants. "You don't take anything seriously."

Jimmy stood in front of a mirror that leaned against the wall. He looked at himself for a moment and then drew his right hand to a mark on his neck.

"And I'm sick of showing up for work with hickeys," Jimmy said. "Do you know how embarrassing that is?"

"I'm sorry," said Michael. "I just get excited."

"But I *told* you not to do it anymore."

"You said no more hickeys on your face. That's what you said."

"This is ridiculous." Jimmy put on his blue work vest emblazoned with the words "Wal*Mart. Always Low Prices."

"You realize I'm in management now," said Jimmy. "I need to be taken seriously. It's bad enough that those jerks in Receiving keep calling me 'the Wal-Douche.'"

Michael tightened his lips to keep from laughing.

"But it's not just that," Jimmy continued. "I feel like I'm at a point in life…I mean, I'm 22. It's time to start acting like a fucking adult."

"Why are you going there with the age thing," Michael said, sitting up. "I can't change how old I am."

"But you can change how you *act*," Jimmy said. "Have you given any more thought to what we talked about last week?"

"About living together? No. I told you I wasn't ready. I'm not ready."

"Well, I need to know this is going somewhere." Jimmy put on his round schoolboy glasses and tried unsuccessfully to smooth down the cowlick that always shot from the back of his head.

"I'm just not ready for all of that yet," Michael said. He paused and grinned. "But I love us together. I love what we just did." Michael pulled Jimmy toward him. "Didn't you think it was amazing?"

Jimmy closed his eyes.

"We could get out the wand," Michael said.

With his glasses and messy hair, Jimmy bore an uncanny resemblance to Harry Potter. In fact, some of their best sex played out like erotic fan fiction with Michael pretending to be a range of characters, from the hot-but-doomed Cedric Diggory to Dobby, the house elf.

"It's not about the wand," Jimmy said, backing away from Michael's grasp. "It's just time for me to move on."

There was a short silence between them as Jimmy continued getting dressed. Then Jimmy walked out of the bedroom, through the living room, and toward the door. Michael followed.

"I don't understand why we can't just chill?" Michael said

Jimmy opened the door. "Michael, when you chill for too long, you start to freeze." Then he slammed the door behind him.

Michael walked back to the bedroom, fell onto the bed, and stared at the white ceiling. He knew that he and Jimmy had issues, but he hadn't seen *this* coming, not a breakup. Michael felt something like a bruise forming in his chest.

In addition to being hurt, he was also embarrassed. Michael was 39-years-old and his 22-year-old boyfriend had just broken up with him for being too immature. Michael wondered how he would break the news to his best friends, Sidney and Bruce. He also wondered if they would ever stop laughing once he did.

Chapter 2

Sidney laughed loudest, a huge bellowing laugh that sprang from his 260-pound frame. His laugh was so loud that it drew the attention of several other people upstairs at the Mirror Ball, the oldest gay bar in Providence, Rhode Island.

"It's really not *that* funny," Michael said.

"Oh no, bitch, it's funny," said Sidney, quaking with laughter. "It's funny as *hell*."

Bruce's laugh was a more restrained chuckle. But since his job as a Johnson and Wales campus cop demanded a certain stoicism, this understated laugh was the equivalent of a spit-spewing guffaw.

The three of them—Michael, Sidney and Bruce—made an odd trio, sitting together at a table near the bar. Sidney, both Michael's best friend and the art dealer who represented his photography, was a rotund, expresso-colored black man in his late 50s, dressed in a plain yet stylish, sweater and slacks. Michael, several shades lighter on the African-American color continuum, was dramatically more casual in dress. His look offered a middle-aged spin on middle school chic—jeans, Chucks, and a vintage t-shirt with the words "I'm Crabby" atop a drawing of a peeved crustacean.

Towering over both of them at more than 6 feet was Bruce, a swarthy, hard-muscled mix of Irish and Italian ancestry, who was the baby at age 33. As always, Bruce's outfit consisted of a high-waisted pair of light-wash Lee's matched with some t-shirt that he had probably gotten for free at a radio-station-sponsored sporting event. He wore his dark hair slicked back in a style that came off either as classic or dated depending on how much Brylcreem he used.

The friendship of Michael, Sidney and Bruce was a byproduct of the Mirror Ball's unique social dynamics. It was one of those gay bars that you only find in smaller cities, a big-tent kind of place that brought together nearly every sub-species of the Modern Homosexual, from fake-ID-wielding teens to seniors; Wendy's fry cooks to university professors, hipsters to homo-thugs, and, in the parlance of hook-up sites, str8-acters to femmes.

"So honestly, did he come right out and say you were too immature for him?" asked Bruce. "Seriously, this 22-year-old twink?"

"He said I *acted* too immature."

"Well, can you blame him?" said Sidney.

"How am I immature?" asked Michael.

"You're so upset that he broke up with you, but at the same time, you don't want something like a real adult relationship. That would require plans and, I don't know, considering someone else's needs for once."

"Maybe I should just fuck hustlers like you?" Michael said, cutting his eyes at Sidney.

"Baby, I represent your work; you can't afford them."

"Just dick 'em and dump 'em." Bruce said.

"I hate hooking up," Michael said. "It's like having to go grocery shopping every time you want to eat. Sometimes you just want something to be in the 'fridge."

"See, that's your problem," Bruce said. "You're in a no-'mo's land, stuck between grindr and, I don't know, two dudes on a cake."

"All I know is that I didn't want to break up," Michael said. "I really didn't want to be alone again."

Bruce stood up. "Well, I'm gonna go walk around so that I'm not alone *tonight*."

This was the pattern of the way Bruce, Michael and Sidney hung out: converge, disperse, converge—repeat until last call.

Michael went to the bar to get another drink. At the end of the bar stood Andy, a "shot boy," who got paid to walk around in his underwear selling test tubes of variously flavored liquor concoctions. A burly University of Rhode Island hockey player, Andy more than filled out the baby blue Calvin Klein briefs he was wearing. He'd been working at the club for several months and there was still fierce debate about whether he was gay or just another straight boy who recognized the financial opportunities inherent in strutting around in his skivvies in front of a bunch of horny homos.

"'Sup?" Andy said as Michael passed.

"Chillin'," Michael answered.

"Where's your boy tonight?" Andy asked.

"We broke up," Michael said. "Well, he broke up with me."

"Sucks," said Andy, adjusting the waistband of his briefs.

"No shit."

"Want a shot to cheer you up?" Andy said, displaying his colorful tray of tubes. "On me."

Michael eyed the tray suspiciously. "I never drink this shit. What's good?"

Andy picked up a cloudy tube of crème-colored liquid. "Well, my favorite is this one. It's called a blow job."

Michael smirked, took the tube from Andy's hand, and downed it in one swift gesture. He grimaced at the taste, like watered-down Kahlua.

"Now you can say that I gave you a blow job," Andy said with a wink before walking away.

Michael ordered his drink, a vodka and Diet Coke, and took the stairs to the second floor, a balcony-like mezzanine where you could look down on the lower level dance floor. Michael loved that the Mirror Ball had three floors. There was always somewhere to go.

As Michael leaned against the wood railing and gazed down upon the flailing bodies and flashing lights, he noticed a guy he'd never seen before. This was a significant occurrence since Providence's gay scene was relatively small and insular. The guy he spotted was a young, skinny kid like any number of the twinks that congregated at the Mirror Ball because of its 18 and up policy. But he stood out primarily because of his hair, which was molded into a 9 inch mohawk.

The Mohawk kid skittered across the dance floor like a startled animal, darting this way and that, knocking into people, spilling drinks. Michael couldn't tell if the kid was headed somewhere or awkwardly trying to dance.

After a couple of minutes, the kid moved away from the dance floor into the shadows near the wall. Every now and then, a swirling light would hit the kid's face and Michael could see his eyes, wide, taking everything in.

Michael was wondering what it would be like for all of this to feel new again, when suddenly two large arms wrapped around his waist.

"What the…" he said, turning around.

It was Bruce, laughing.

"And you fucking call me immature?" Michael said.

Bruce leaned against the wooden railing and draped an arm over Michael's shoulder. "You're not gonna jump, are ya?"

"Fuck off."

"No, it'd be a pretty awesome way to go, splattered on the dance floor."

"I'm not suicidal, dick. I'm just down. You would know what that was like if you actually had feelings."

Bruce shrugged. "Who's the new kid?" he asked, pointing below.

"What new kid?" Michael said, even though he knew exactly who Bruce was talking about.

Bruce pointed at the Mohawk kid who had moved back onto the dance floor. "That one."

"Never seen him before."

"He's cute." Bruce watched the kid for a while. "His hair is all kinds of fucked up. But he's cute."

"I don't even fucking care," Michael said.

"See, that's your problem," Bruce said. "Jimmy broke up with you. Nothing you can do about it. Move on."

"Dude, it was this afternoon."

"Regardless—"

"That's why I liked having a boyfriend. It put an end to all this...all this looking."

"That's the fun of it."

"Well, it's not fun for me, not anymore."

They stayed silent for a few minutes. The crowd undulated below. One pounding song merged into the next.

"It sucks being dumped," Michael said. "It just does. When Jimmy told me he wanted to break up, I felt like I was being kicked off a reality show, like RuPaul was gonna sweep into the room and tell me to 'sashay away'."

"I don't watch that *Drag Race* shit," Bruce said.

Michael rolled his eyes.

"You know what show I used to watch, though?" Bruce said.

"No fucking idea."

"*Flavor of Love*. Now that shit used to crack me up. I even started giving my tricks nicknames like Flav."

"You can't be serious."

"I never told you that?" Bruce said and then pointed to a tall, gangly kid on the dancefloor. "See that one?"

Michael nodded.

"Inchez, enormous tool."

"I thought you were strictly a top."

"Don't mean I can't appreciate a big dick." Bruce said. Then he pointed to a short kid with curly, ginger hair. "Oh God, that one's Fartz. It was like fucking a squeak toy."

Bruce's eyes continued scanning the crowd. "Molez," he said, his finger directed at a pale, reed-thin guy in a Brown t-shirt. "You should see his back."

Michael nodded.

"Oh and him over there, the blond?"

Michael nodded again.

"Zitz. You should see his ass."

Michael laughed.

"O.K., see the short guy dancing on the box, the one who keeps giving me the eye."

"Yeah," Michael said.

"His sack is enormous," Bruce said, making a large circle with his hands. "It's kinda freaky, but he's a good lay."

"Lemme guess," Michael said. "Ballz?".

Bruce responded, "Nutz."

Closing time approached and Michael walked back upstairs to find Sidney, who was getting ready to leave. "Let's go before they turn on the lights in this bitch," Sidney said. "Do you need a ride?"

"No, I think I want to walk tonight," Michael said.

They made their way outside and through the cigarette-smoking crowd that was gathered around the entrance. The smoke, the streetlights, and the World War II-era building that housed the Mirror Ball gave the scene a film-like ambiance: homo noir.

"Bye, baby," Sidney said, giving Michael a hug. "You sure you don't want a ride?"

"Yeah, I'm sure," Michael said.

"O.K., well, be safe," said Sidney, as he walked to his cream-colored BMW parked across the street. Just before closing the car door, he yelled back to Michael: "Go watch some 19-year-old Russian jerk off on Chaturbate. That always cheers you up."

Michael laughed, and Sidney's car moved down the street. For a moment, Michael looked for Bruce, but he didn't see him. He did, however, catch the Mohawk Kid leaning against the side of the club talking to Zitz. The Mohawk Kid grabbed

Bruce's complexion-challenged friend by the belt and started making out with him.

Michael watched for a couple of moments. The sight made him wonder when he would kiss someone again? He knew this was just a silly post-break-up thought. But at the same time, he was getting older. At some point in life, there must come a time when you've kissed all the guys you're ever gonna kiss. He wondered how much time he had before that moment came for him.

Michael began his journey home. He loved walking through Providence at night, passing the old warehouses, the aging signs for stores that had long since been boarded up, and the weathered brick parking garages that emitted dim yellow glows. The city was battered yet beautiful, and its scars were never more stunning than at night.

Michael arrived at his apartment on Benefit Street, walked straight into the bedroom and stepped out of his jeans. He tossed them toward the clothes hamper in the closet. They did a spectacular leap through the air, but just missed the plastic hamper. Michael rolled his eyes at this latest display of bad luck.

He was just about to plug his phone in the wall, when he decided to check Facebook one last time for the night. He knew it was a desperate act, but Jimmy often wrote goodnight messages on his wall. Maybe Jimmy had had a change of heart.

But as soon as he signed in, the first thing he saw on his news feed was "Jimmy Ivers status has changed from 'in a relationship' to 'single.'

Chapter 3

Several blocks away, down Benefit Street and onto
Wickenden Street, two figures stumbled in the dark. The taller of
the two turned to steady the shorter, less steady one.

"We're almost there," Bruce said, as they climbed the
hilly street, walking past a coffee house, a thrift shop, two Italian
restaurants, and—in keeping with Providence's reputation as the
Red Light District of New England—a sex shop.

"I want you…," Bruce's shorter, younger companion
began, before his speech was interrupted by a belch. "Sorry," he
continued, waving his hand in front of his mouth. "I fucking

want you to fuck me so fucking hard," he said and then belched again.

"Be quiet," Bruce said in a hoarse whisper. He grabbed the arm of the guy he'd nicknamed "Nutz" and hurried him along. He didn't move too quickly though, because he didn't want Nutz to barf. Bruce was out of spare toothbrushes, and it was so distracting to have to dodge a guy's mouth all night when you were trying to fuck him. Bruce made a mental note to pick up toothbrushes the next time he was at the Dollar Tree.

"And use your handcuffs like last time," Nutz continued, bouncing slightly to ensure that his words reached Bruce's ears. "And leave your work boots on…"

The two continued up the hill, past a Cambodian restaurant and a head shop. They turned a corner and soon stood in front of Bruce's two greatest loves—his white, three-story house and the blue Ford pickup truck parked alongside it.

"Stay right here," Bruce said as they stood on the sidewalk. He looked directly into Nutz's glassy brown eyes. "I'm serious. Don't fucking move."

Bruce ensured that Nutz was steady, then he dashed over to his truck, unlocked the door, and fished around for something on the floor. After he closed the truck door, quietly, he turned and saw Nutz rapidly making his way up the front stairs. Bruce raced over and stopped Nutz's hand just as he was about to knock on the door. "I told you to fucking stay where you were," Bruce said. He spun Nutz around and gripped his arms.

"Oh my God," Nutz said. "I have such wood right now."

Bruce led Nutz back down the stairs, then around the side of the house to a back entrance. Motion sensor lights clicked on, and for a moment, the handcuffs dangling from Bruce's backpocket gleamed in the night.

#

About a half mile away, in an apartment that overlooked downtown Providence, Sidney Burke was breaking a promise to himself. He held his iPhone in his hand and shuffled through the contacts until he came upon the name Dante. He waited a beat, took a long breath, and then pressed the name. He hoped he wasn't making a mistake.

As the phone tried to connect, Sidney wondered why it bothered him so much that he was breaking his policy of never seeing the same escort more than a few times. He knew the rule was silly in a way. But somehow it helped him maintain a sense of perspective about the whole sex-for-money thing. He refused to be one of those pitiable saps who fooled themselves into thinking that a paid hookup was an actual relationship.

When Sidney made the decision to start hiring hustlers, it was not because of some middle-aged feeling that his sexual opportunities were drying up. Far from it. It was rather that, at his age, just south of sixty, he was increasingly tired, resentful even, of the time and energy it took to negotiate even the most basic sexual encounter. At a club, there was the whole eyes-meeting-across-the-room thing, followed by forced repartee that seldom reached the level of wit, and then the waiting around until last call to take the guy home only to find out that he was either too drunk to fuck or so bad at fucking that the whole ordeal was a waste of time.

Sidney knew this approach was old school, because most guys hooked up on their phones these days. But Sidney found all the texting back and forth to be exasperating. It made him feel like a harried switchboard operator in a screwball comedy from the '40s.

Hiring a hustler was far more pleasant and efficient. Sidney took care of his sexual needs in the same manner that he tended to his other needs: getting his hair cut, regular manicures and pedicures, a weekly massage. Sidney would find a guy that he liked on RentMe.com, and shortly thereafter, the guy of his choice would be at his door. It was as efficient—and frankly as tasty—as his favorite Thai delivery.

Sidney loved being at a place in life where he could control and regulate his sexual encounters. He wasn't like Michael, who could spend months flirting with the same twink without once ever sticking his dick in the kid's orthodontically enhanced mouth. Sidney needed sex to function. He needed to feel the resistance upon entering a guy's body and then the subsequent ecstatic release.

He also needed novelty. He wasn't looking for "The Boyfriend Experience," a designation that popped up in so many RentMe ads these days; he wanted the disposable "Boy Toy

Experience." He desired variety in sex in the same way that he liked it in other areas of his life.

But tonight marked the fifth time that he'd called Dante. This was a record.

"Hello," Dante answered, sleepily. But then Sidney often thought Dante sounded sleepy. It was all a part of the laidback attitude that Sidney found so sexy.

"It's Sidney. Sidney Burke."

"I know it's you."

"I was calling to ask if you wanted…or rather, if you were available to come over?"

"Yes, I want to come over," Dante said, sounding more alert.

"Good," Sidney said. "I'm glad you're free. I'll leave word with the doorman."

"It will take me about 30 minutes."

"See you when you get here."

Sidney spent the next half hour making sure everything in the condo was in order. He clicked on the light in the guest bedroom where he always took his boys-for-hire. He ran one finger along the mahogany nightstand. The housekeeper was sometimes lax about dusting this room, and Sidney hated to be distracted by stray detritus when he was trying to bust a nut.

Once he felt the room was to his liking, Sidney took a small key and unlocked a cabinet in the nightstand. He looked through the top shelf of the cabinet, which contained plenty of his favorite brand of condoms—Magnums—and lube—Gun Oil. He also was relieved to see that he was still well-stocked in Listerine breath strips, Wet Wipes, tissues, and extra absorbent, select-a-size paper towels.

Sidney closed the cabinet and walked to his office, where he controlled the Sonos music system that played throughout the apartment. Sidney enjoyed fucking to Sade, but most of the younger guys he'd hire either had never heard of her or they'd say something mood shattering like "My mom used to listen to her." So, Sidney thought, "fuck it," and put on Sam Smith.

Sidney was sitting in his living room, flipping through the latest issue of *Artforum*, when the doorbell rang. He got up, opened the door, and saw Dante standing there, thin but sturdy, in a zip-up hoodie and jeans. His skin was a deep, polished-wood brown, and his eyelashes were so long that they almost seemed fake.

Sidney let Dante into the condo. They exchanged greetings and the kind of hug you might give a co-worker at a Christmas party. Sidney was always cautious about being too affectionate with a rentboy before the clock officially started ticking. He didn't need to pretend that they were old friends or two guys meeting for a date. This was sex and business.

"I'm glad you called," Dante said.

"Why?" Sidney said. He motioned for Dante to follow him into the guest bedroom.

"I like when we hang out."

"Is that what this is called these days," Sidney asked as he entered the spare bedroom and sat on the bed, "hanging out?"

"You can call it whatever you want to call it," Dante said. He positioned his body between Sidney's open legs and ran his fingers along the sides of Sidney's face.

Sidney looked into Dante's eyes. "I just don't like pretending that shit is what it ain't."

"Then what is it?" Dante asked. He placed his right thumb on Sidney's chin.

"Business," Sidney said. His hands moved between Dante's thighs and gripped Dante's steadily stiffening cock.

"What if I told you I would've come for free?" Dante asked.

"I would tell you that my momma didn't raise no fool."

Dante dropped to his knees and started unzipping Sidney's pants.

"Do you want to know why I like hanging out with you?" Dante asked.

Sidney paused. "Can you tell me with my dick in your mouth?"

#

Approximately 100 miles away, Traci Hunter was driving down a rainy stretch of I-95. One hand steered the car, while the other dove into a bag of trail mix. She grabbed a fistful of the mix and aimed it toward her mouth. But the mass of raisins, almonds, and sunflower seeds sorely missed their intended target. "Shit," Traci said, as she tried to brush the debris from her sweatshirt.

Her free hand bumped the steering wheel and her Volvo went swerving on a patch of wet pavement. The car skidded into the next lane, and the basketball-sized headlights of an 18-wheeler charged toward her.

An image popped into her mind. It was of her son Ziggy in his new dorm room at the Rhode Island School of Design. She saw him as clearly as if his image was being projected on her windshield: the spiky jet black mohawk; the dark brown eyes that always seemed both a little angry and a little sad; the subtle variations of his near ubiquitous scowl.

She thought, Ziggy had been fatherless since he was born and now he was about to be motherless. This made her feel guilty in more ways that she'd ever want to admit.

But the image of her son faded quickly, as her attention snapped back to the more immediate matter at hand. She jerked the steering wheel to the right, and, thank God, her car crossed back into the correct lane and then onto the gravelly shoulder. She jammed her foot onto the brake pedal, and the car lurched to a stop. The 18-wheeler zoomed past, its horn issuing an indignant honk.

With her heart thumping, Traci pulled back on the highway and grasped another handful of trail mix. She knew she should stop eating it. She'd already used up her entire daily allotment of Weight Watcher Plus points, and the trail mix was doing nothing to help with the 10 pounds she wanted to lose by…well, that she *always* wanted to lose. But at this point, it was the only thing keeping her going.

This was Traci's sixth hour on the road from Providence, RI. to Takoma Park, MD, outside of Washington D.C. She wondered how it was going to feel coming home knowing that Ziggy wouldn't be returning for months. For all intents and purposes, she was now living alone.

When she told people that Ziggy was going away to school, they either gave her a pitying look or immediately began suggesting guys they could hook her up with. So far, she'd turned down every one of these so-called opportunities. It wasn't that she was opposed to seeing someone. But she didn't feel like having it become yet another thing on her to-do list.

The only guy she was remotely interested in was Lionel, a reporter who worked with her in the "Style" section at *The Washington Post*. They had recently bonded at a John Legend concert. But there were rumors that Lionel was gay, and she had to admit that he did seem to over-identify with some of the *Real Housewives of Atlanta*.

Traci hadn't responded to his last few texts. Her days of dealing with sexually ambiguous guys were way behind her—like back in college.

The only gay guy in her life now was her son. She discovered Ziggy's sexual orientation when he was in second grade. They were at a birthday party for another boy in Ziggy's class. Ziggy ran around with the kids outside, while Traci sat in the living room with the other parents debating the appropriateness of Britney Spears as a role model. Some of the mothers were still smarting from Britney's MTV snake dance, not to mention her sporting a sparkly nude bodysuit in her recent "Toxic" video. Traci argued that she didn't see anything wrong with Britney. She was just this generation's female pop provocateur a la Madonna. Traci added that Ziggy adored Britney.

As if on cue, Ziggy walked into the room and publicly announced what he wanted to be when he grew up. "I want to be a doctor," he proclaimed, his hair sticking up on top of his head even then. Traci filled with pride. Instantaneously, she felt freed from all those dire prognostications about the bleak prospects of the children of single mothers.

"That's wonderful, honey" she said, as she tried to smooth down his hair. "You want to make sick people better?"

He pulled back from her reach. "No, no," he laughed. "I want to play with pee-pees."

Traci's jaw went slack. She imagined all of the other mother's now judging her and her liberal Britney-approving ways.

This was just the beginning of the journey Traci would take to understand her son's sexuality. This struggle had nothing to do with Ziggy being gay, but more that he was so fundamentally different from every other gay man she'd known.

As soon as Traci recovered from the shock and embarrassment of the birthday party revelation, she committed herself to becoming the most supportive mother she could be. She joined Parents and Friends of Lesbians and Gays. She relearned the lyrics to "William's Doll" from *Free to Be...You and Me*. And she began giving serious thought to how she was going to help Ziggy cope with some of the harsher realities of growing up gay, things she'd learned from gay friends in college during late night confessionals. She'd have to tell Ziggy what to do when someone called him a gay slur. And she'd have to be there to comfort him on all those dateless nights, or that moment when the straight boy of his dreams carelessly broke his heart. (She had heard *that* story from so many different gay guys that she sometimes felt it had happened to her.) She planned to do whatever it took to keep him safe in mind, body, and spirit. She saw herself as a fierce momma lion protecting her limp-pawed cub.

But Ziggy failed to meet any of her expectations. Far from being a stay-indoors, play-with-Barbies type, Ziggy was a jump-out-of-trees, skateboard-down-the-staircase kind of boy. It also quickly became clear that he could more than protect himself. In the 6th grade, a fellow student, Terry McGraw, had teased Ziggy about not having a dad. Ziggy punched Terry in the face and knocked out one of his baby teeth. After that, no other kid dared mess with him.

As for his romantic life, Ziggy was never much for dating. But that didn't mean he wasn't highly libidinous, much to Traci's frequent chagrin—all the sticky underwear and socks and sheets and washcloths and hand towels, etc… Even Ziggy's art had a sexual element. It mostly entailed canvases splattered with blood, spit, snot, and that other more rambunctious bodily fluid. On some level, Traci was just glad it was no longer landing on her linens. His work won him a scholarship to the Rhode Island School of Design, commonly referred to as RISD, which was one of the most prestigious art colleges in the country.

Traci was thoroughly proud of Ziggy. But the rawness of the work unsettled her. It made her feel like she should be protecting him in some way that she'd yet to think of. The hardest part about mothering Ziggy was knowing which parts of him needed to be mothered. Even as a little boy, he rarely showed his soft places and when he did, they were already bruised or stained with blood.

Traci couldn't help but be concerned about his move to Providence. Of course, she was worried about the general kid-going-to-college stuff: would he do well; would he keep safe; would he ever call home? But these weren't the things causing the undercurrent of anxiety that she'd been living with since Ziggy announced his intention to go to RISD.

What she feared most was that he'd uncover a secret she'd been keeping since his birth, the secret that his father wasn't some anonymous purveyor of lab-quality spunk but rather her former college buddy—and the source of much of what she knew about gay men—Michael Allen.

Back at the University of Maryland at College Park, they had the whole gay boy/straight girl friendship thing going on, until one night after a Janet Jackson concert, woozy from one too many Zimas, they decided to "do it." The result was so awkward and unsatisfying that they never mentioned it again.

Three months later, Traci found herself in the bathroom of her mother's house holding a plastic strip with a window that had just turned blue. Several months later, she was a mom.

Traci never told anyone who the father was, but she led people to believe that it was a married professor. She felt so overwhelmed by the thought of caring for a new life that she didn't want to have to negotiate parenthood with another person, especially Michael, who, while sweet, was more than a bit immature. She couldn't imagine that he'd be able to cope with something as life changing as fatherhood, and more important, she didn't feel like walking him through it.

Occasionally, she felt guilty about keeping this secret, not so much for Michael, who she was convinced was better off not knowing, but for Ziggy. When he was old enough to start asking about his father, she concocted a story about him being a test tube baby. After a while, it seemed like he carried this as a badge of honor. But there were other times when she knew that not having a father bothered him. Toothless Terry McGraw learned that all too well.

As for Michael, Traci rarely spoke to him after that. But she did occasionally Google him just to keep up with his whereabouts. His photography website stated that he was now based in Providence, which is what made her a little nervous about the Ziggy situation. But then she thought, of course, she was being silly. Surely gay men in their late 30s don't run in the same circles as 19-year-olds. Do they?

Part Two

Chapter 4

Several weeks later, on a chilly October evening, Sidney

walked through his apartment lighting lemongrass-scented

candles. Sade's "Love is Stronger than Pride" played in the

background. He moved to his living room window, which

stretched from the floor to the ceiling, and opened the blinds.

The twinkling Providence skyline smiled at him. He breathed

deeply, exhaled.

In about half an hour, Dante was supposed to be there.

Sidney had been seeing Dante about once a week for more than a

month now. They'd been together so many times that Sidney had

stopped keeping count. On most nights, they'd retreat into the guest bedroom for sex. Dante would press his back against the headboard, and, in a move that reflected his high school gymnastic training, raise his muscled legs into a flying V. Sidney would grab hold of Dante' thick thighs and fuck him steady and deep.

Indeed all of this regular sex had given Sidney's biceps and thighs an increased firmness. He'd even lost 10 pounds in the process. Sidney wondered if, at his next check-up, he should tell his doctor that he'd increased both his cardio and resistance training.

Sometimes he and Dante wouldn't even have sex. Instead, they'd spend the evening sitting on the living-room couch, eating popcorn and watching *Charlie Rose*. They'd fall asleep with Dante's head cradled underneath Sidney's right arm.

By all appearances, things were getting quite domestic, that is except for the envelope filled with five $50 bills that Sidney always put on a small table by the door. Dante still hinted that he would see Sidney even if money weren't involved, yet he always slipped the envelope into his messenger bag as he walked out the door.

Tonight, the plan was for them to start with a light snack of crabmeat bruschetta. Sidney figured this would give them a nice protein boost before they headed into the bedroom. The only problem was that Sidney had forgotten the bread. He'd asked Dante to pick some up on the way over.

Sidney was lighting a candle in the kitchen, when his phone rang. It was the front desk. Sidney thought this was strange since he'd already left word for the doorman to send Dante up.

"Charlie, what's up?," Sidney asked the doorman.

"A 'Michael Allen' is here to see you," Charlie answered.

"What the fuck is he doing here?" Sidney thought.

Charlie continued: "And since he wasn't the person you previously said would be—"

"That's quite alright," Sidney said, not wanting him to go any further. Charlie was great when it came to receiving packages, arranging for dry cleaning, and dealing with maintenance issues, but he left much to be desired in terms of discretion.

"Just send him up," Sidney said sharply.

"Right away, Mr. Burke."

Sidney wondered again why Michael was there. He knew Michael had been in Manhattan for the day, meeting with magazine editors to drum up some photography work. But Sidney figured they'd debrief tomorrow. Something must have gone wrong, which meant Michael would want to talk. But Sidney had no time to talk. He didn't want Michael to run into Dante. He didn't want to have to explain his "thing" with Dante. He wasn't sure he understood it himself.

"Hey," Michael said flatly, as Sidney opened the door. He gave Sidney a weak hug and then walked into the kitchen. He placed a black portfolio on the counter, sighed, and sat on a barstool.

"I take it that things in New York didn't go as planned," Sidney said.

Michael again let out a loud sigh.

"What happened?" Sidney asked.

"Nothing happened," Michael said. "That's the problem. It's the same old shit. People said they liked my work, but that it wasn't right for them right now, that it's too personal, that it doesn't fit their direction."

"As I've told you," Sidney said, "you just have to keep doing what you're doing and eventually the editorial people will come around. In the meantime, you have plenty of patrons who love your work."

Michael sighed dramatically.

"The magazine world always lags behind the art world," Sidney explained. "But pretty soon they'll be throwing money at you just to take a shot of Zac Efron's ass. Have faith."

As Sidney spoke, he flipped through Michael's portfolio. Page after page, there were beautiful young men moodily looking back at him. They preened and flexed for the camera; gave it the finger; spat at it; clouded it with cigarette smoke. Michael juxtaposed these pictures with more intimate images—a guy grinned while sitting on the toilet, another lay naked in the afternoon sun. Then there was one photo—perhaps one of Michael's best—where a tattooed blond tough guy gently blew the camera a kiss. This mix of bravado and vulnerability was the defining characteristic of Michael's work. Technically, his pictures could be a blurry, grainy, out-of-focus mess. But the soul of the work was undeniable.

Sidney knew that he needed to wrap the conversation up. But with the portfolio still open to the picture of the tattooed man-boy, Sidney couldn't help but ask, "Have you heard from Chase lately?"

"No," Michael said, slumping on the stool.

Sidney saw Michael's wounded look and instantly regretted bringing Chase up. Sidney closed the portfolio.

"I really think you need to go home and get a good night's sleep," Sidney said. "Start fresh tomorrow. Everything will look different."

"Let's go out," Michael said with a jolt.

"What?" Sidney said.

"Seriously, let's go to Mirror Ball."

"Now? Tonight? No way." Sidney said. "I've had a long day; you've had a long day."

"Exactly," Michael said. "At this point, it won't make any difference if we stay up a little longer. We'll be just as tired in the morning."

Michael blew out the candle on the counter. "Come on, you're already dressed."

"No," Sidney said, grabbing an electric lighter from a drawer and reigniting the candle. "I'm in for the night."

"No, seriously," Michael said, grabbing the candle from Sidney's hand and snuffing it out again. "I really need to go out."

Sidney felt an almost physical sensation of his patience leaving him. "What you need to do is stop fucking with my candles," he said, snatching the candle back from Michael and lighting it again. "Then you need to go home. Nothing good happens when you're in one of your moods."

"What do you mean 'my moods'?"

"You're gonna go to the club, wanting to cheer up," Sidney said. "But something's not gonna go the way you wanted it to and you'll be more miserable than before."

"I'm not *that* bad."

"I've seen it happen too many times," Sidney said. "And if I had wanted to see a disaster tonight, I would've streamed *Titanic* on Netflix.'"

Michael rolled his eyes and turned toward the crabmeat brushetta. "That looks great," Michael said. "I'm starving."

"No," Sidney said, grabbing the container out of Michael's reach. "I'm out of bread, and, besides, I'm going to sleep."

"This is how it starts, you know," Michael said.

"What?" Sidney snapped.

"This is how it starts, the whole getting-old-and-not-going-out-anymore thing. It's a slippery slope. You start staying in a couple of nights in a row and the next thing you know, you're one of those trolls who only go to the club on weekends. You know, the ones who wear cardigans and dad jeans pulled up to the nads."

"Look," Sidney said, "unlike you, I'm not afraid of getting older, so I don't have some pathological need to go out every night to prove that I can still hang. And furthermore—"

Michael interrupted, looking at the Sub-Zero refrigerator. "Do you have any water? All your bitching is making me thirsty."

Sidney opened the refrigerator, grabbed a small bottle of San Pellegrino and handed it to Michael. "Take it to go."

"You can be so mean," Michael said, opening the bottle and taking a long swig. "I can't believe you won't go out with me on a night like tonight, when I *need* you."

"Text Bruce," Sidney said. He'll go out with you."

"I already tried. He's staying in too."

"Why?"

"I don't know. You know how vague his texts are. He just wrote 'not goin' out.' That could mean anything from being sleepy to having a 12-way with the Brown University rowing team."

Sidney's iPhone buzzed in his pocket. While Michael took another gulp of water, Sidney looked at the screen. It was a text from Dante: "Be there in 5."

"So, anyway," Sidney said. "Go home. Get some sleep."

Michael huffed.

"It will all be better tomorrow," Sidney continued, picking up Michael's portfolio from the counter and handing it to him. "You know what the Bible says, 'joy comes in the morning' and all of that."

Michael raised his eyebrows. "Seriously? That is the least inspirational use of a Bible verse *ever*."

"Well, baby, that's all you're getting tonight."

Michael looked at the time on his phone: "Hey, 'Watch What Happens Live' is about to come on. Why don't we—"

"Motherfucker, get out!"

"O.K." Michael said, getting up from the stool. "You don't have to be such a dick about it."

Michael put his portfolio back on the counter. "But keep this," Michael said. "I don't want to take it to the club."

Sidney nodded, as he walked Michael to the door.

"You know I love you," Sidney said.

"I know."

Sidney pulled Michael into a tight hug and patted him on the back. "Now get the fuck out."

Chapter 5

Michael was leaving Sidney's building, when he passed

an attractive young man with walnut-colored skin and strikingly

long eyelashes. The guy carried a brown paper bag with a roll of

French bread protruding from the top. Michael held the door

open for the guy and exchanged a friendly nod. After the door

closed, Michael glanced behind him to see if the guy was also

looking his way, the universal signal of carnal homosexual

intent. But the young man was already standing in an open

elevator, and the shiny elevator doors quickly closed.

Michael headed down Exchange Street and over the

bridge across the Providence River. The river, which could look rather dank in the daylight, came alive with flashes of reflected light at night. As Michael crossed Memorial Boulevard, with the red neon sign for the Biltmore Hotel shining in front of him like a beacon, his thoughts turned to Chase. This probably would've happened even if Sidney hadn't mentioned him earlier. Michael simply couldn't walk through the city without thinking about the person who helped him fall in love with it.

Michael arrived in Providence a few years ago at Sidney's suggestion. He and Sidney knew each other from the New York art scene. At the time, Michael was a photo editor at *Entertainment Weekly* magazine, but he took his own pictures on the side. Michael frequented the city's many photography galleries, where he'd often run into Sidney. Though Sidney's gallery was based in Providence, he made frequent trips to New York to keep up with the latest art world happenings.

One day, they were both at a Soho gallery admiring some Keizo Kitajimas when Michael asked if Sidney would look at some of his work. Michael had been building up the nerve to ask for months. He felt like he needed some feedback and direction, but he didn't want to approach any of the New York gallery owners because he saw them all the time. Sidney lived out of town, so he was a safer bet.

Sidney agreed to take a glance at his work, so they met up at a Starbucks on 10th Avenue. Michael was tense, anxious, and uncharacteristically quiet as he watched Sidney flip through his portfolio. It consisted mostly of photos of strippers that Michael met as they passed through town doing engagements at the now defunct Times Square theater the Gaiety. Michael's pictures captured the guys in various states of undress, lounging around their budget hotel rooms; napping before shows; eating pizza in their underwear; smoking weed and drinking 40s.

Sidney flipped through the pictures slowly. He stopped on one photo of a naked guy sitting in a bathtub filled with water; tears streamed down his face.

"What's the story here?" Sidney asked.

Michael looked at the photo. "Oh him? He was Canadian. Lots of guys who stripped at the Gaiety came down from Canada. When I took this, he had just found out that his girlfriend had given birth to their baby. She wasn't due for another week. He'd been hoping to make it back in time. He wanted to leave as soon as he got the baby news, but he couldn't afford to miss his stint at the Gaiety. It was pretty sad. He was only 19."

Sidney made a "hmmm" sound and flipped to another page.

"So, what do you think, like, overall?" Michael asked, tentatively.

Sidney didn't answer right away. Michael's palms moistened.

"I guess the thing I'm curious about is where you see all of this going." Sidney said. "Is photography just some hobby or—"

"No," Michael interrupted. He leaned forward with such force that he almost toppled his Skinny Vanilla Latte. "It's not a hobby at all. It's all I want to do. I want to be an artist. I mean, I am an artist. But I want to do it full-time. I want this to be my life."

"Well," Sidney sighed, "the one thing I do know…and excuse me if I'm blunt, but that's my nature. The one thing I do know is that you'll never be the artist you want to be if you stay in New York."

Michael's mouth dropped open. "What do you mean? People move to the city every day to become artists?"

"That's not the point," Sidney said. "Look, your work is good. But in order to achieve what you want, in order to create a body of work that means something, you need to commit to it wholly. It can't be an after work or weekend thing. It has to be your whole day; it has to *be* your life."

"Why can't I do that in New York?"

"Oh, come on," Sidney chuckled. "One thing you'll learn about me is that I don't bullshit. I know so many people like you. People who came to New York wanting to focus on their art, but then took some corporate job to make ends meet. You're a photo editor, right?"

Michael nodded.

"So you spend all day looking at *other* photographers' work, am I right?" Sidney said.

Michael nodded again.

"And you've been working at the job for several years now?"

Another nod from Michael.

"And you're probably making a fairly decent salary after years of being broke?"

More nodding.

"You probably have a fairly decent place now. You dine out regularly—"

"What's your point?" Michael almost shouted.

"My point is, how are you gonna give that up? Are you really gonna quit your day job and go live in some squalid dump in Queens, slurping ramen from a cup and sleeping with bedbugs? Are you really willing to give up the comforts of the life you have for the uncertainty of the life you want?"

Michael had an indigestion-like sensation in his stomach.

"It's just too hard to start over in Manhattan," Sidney continued. "There are too many incentives not to."

Michael didn't say anything. But in his mind, he went through the list of all of his New York media friends who talked about wanting to do something different, something more personal and artistic. He couldn't think of a single one who was doing it.

Sidney went on: "If you really want to become an artist, one who matters, you need to go someplace where you can commit yourself to it. Someplace where you can change without being constantly reminded of what you've giving up. Hell, someplace like Providence. It's cheap and has a strong artistic community—"

"Do you think I can do it, be an artist?" Michael asked, softly.

"I don't know the answer to that," Sidney said, taking a long sip from his Venti Americano. "But if you stay in New York, *you'll* never know either."

A couple of months later, Michael emailed Sidney with plans for his imminent move to Providence. He also asked if Sidney would represent his photography; Sidney agreed.

In Michael's mind, he was making the move for art. But there were other motivations that he couldn't quite articulate to himself, much less to others. It wasn't that these feelings were hard to face. They were just hard to get hold of.

Professionally, Michael was moving up the masthead as a photo editor. He liked what he did. But did he love it? He wasn't sure. Working at *Entertainment Weekly* had become more than a job; it was a habit—going to the same building each day; dealing with the same people; executing the same sets of tasks with skill but not passion.

Michael had learned quickly that bringing passion to a day job was a dangerous proposition. It was like professing love on a first date—the sentiment would almost surely go unreturned and would set the stage for later heartbreak.

On the personal front, Michael just couldn't get anything going. His whole romantic life seemed to be a succession of first dates that never led to second ones. It was maddening. Statistically, it seemed almost impossible *not* to have a boyfriend in Manhattan. The island was chockfull of successful and attractive gay men. But the reality was that it was a city of "catches" intent on never getting caught.

This situation had a numbing effect on Michael that, in many ways, was more damaging than a broken heart. Michael's very belief in love was eroding. He imagined that one day it wouldn't exist at all.

These feelings played into Michael's decision to move to Providence. He felt like he was giving life another chance to surprise him. On one of his first nights in town, he stood on the Wickenden St. bridge, looking at the towers of the Manchester Power Station aglow with yellow light and exhaling bursts of smoke. He thought about what he'd learned from Googling "Providence" on his phone, that the city's name meant "the protective care of God."

Michael's first weeks in town were a blur of acclimations and adjustments. Once he located his apartment, a one-bedroom in a brick house on Benefit Street that sat a few blocks from Brown University, he had to get the cable, the internet, and the electricity turned on. Then he needed to figure out things like where to do his laundry, the closest theater to catch a movie, and an inexpensive sushi joint that wouldn't leave him with the runs. Sometimes he found the process exciting, but other times it made him retreat beneath his fuzziest, pill-ridden blanket, wishing he were sick so he'd have a legitimate reason not to leave the bed.

His rapidly diminishing savings also weighed on him in those early days was. He'd stopped paying his credit card and student loan bills in order to make his money stretch longer. Luckily Sidney was quickly able to sell about a dozen of Michael's nudes to a gay couple in California. That helped his financial situation from becoming dire.

His personal life in those early days was so personal that it only involved himself. He knew no one in Providence except for Sidney. Several days went by when the only things he said to another person were "tall skinny vanilla latte; extra hot; no foam." One time at the Starbucks on Thayer, he'd actually had to clear his throat before ordering, because it had been more than 48 hours since he'd uttered a word. When his voice came out, it was loud and croaky. It reminded him of the first blast of water from a previously closed spigot.

Sidney called Michael from time to time and invited him to go out to a bar, but Michael usually declined. Part of him wanted to get used to the idea of being alone. Increasingly, he suspected that it might be the way he'd spend the rest of his life.

Michael would walk along Waterplace Park and feel a special kinship with the older men he'd spot sitting by themselves on park benches, staring out onto the river. "That will be me one day," he thought.

In fact, it was on a day like that when he met Chase. Michael was watching an old man feeding pigeons and wondering if one day he would be able to pull off the man's combo of a forest-green, buttoned-down cardigan, brown Rockports, and tan, perma-press trousers. Then something caught Michael's eye. He spotted a young blond guy with a buzz cut walking down Water Street. There was a give-no-fucks swagger to the way the guy moved. Some sensation, almost as if there was a small magnet in his chest, made Michael follow the guy.

Michael walked slowly so that he wouldn't be noticed. He followed as the guy made his way past the back of the

Heritage Building into an alley. Michael stopped and waited a few beats before also he entered the alley. When he looked down the brick-lined path, he saw the guy, spray can in hand, starting to tag a wall.

Michael reached for his camera, which he always carried with him on his walks, and pressed the viewfinder against his eye. But just as he was about to take a picture, the guy turned and started rushing toward Michael saying, "What the fuck are you doing?"

"What?" Michael said, moving the camera from his face and griping it tightly.

"What the fuck are you doing?" the guy repeated, emphasizing each word as if Michael were foreign or learning disabled.

"Nothing," Michael said, backing away.

"The fuck you were," the guy spit, putting the spray can in his backpack. "You were taking my picture."

He moved closer to Michael.

"Are you a cop?" he asked.

Michael took a couple more steps back. He knew he should be scared, but for some reason he wasn't. There was something in the guy's eyes that made Michael feel more curious than threatened, and the guy was gorgeous, a baby-faced bad boy—exactly Michael's type.

"If I were a cop, you'd probably be arrested by now." Michael said.

"Who said you could take my fuckin' picture?"

"Who said you could tag this wall?"

"This your building?" the guy challenged.

"No."

"Then shut the fuck—"

The guy's face froze. He mouthed, "Oh shit!"

Michael turned around and saw that a uniformed cop had entered the alley. He was too far away to see the wet paint on the wall. But it wouldn't be long before he figured out what was going on.

"I gotta get out of here," the guy said to Michael, as he started toward South Main. "You live around here?"

"Yeah, up the hill on Benefit."

"Let's go. Fast!"

They walked briskly uphill and turned onto Benefit Street. Block after block passed in a tense, silent blur. Michael's heart was beating so fast that it reminded him of the time a friend convinced him to try CrossFit. As they walked, Michael kept sneaking glances at his companion who had the intense focused expression of someone concentrating on a test.

After another block or so, it became clear that the cop hadn't followed them. The tension between the two eased.

"I'm Michael, by the way."

"Chase," the guy said, extending his hand.

Their pace slowed as they walked down a block of wooden, pastel-colored dwellings that dated back to the 1700s.

"You live on the East Side?" Michael asked.

"Nah," Chase laughed. "Too rich for my blood."

"Federal Hill?"

"Nope," Chase said. Then he broke out into his best N.W.A.-era Ice Cube impression: "Straight outta Cranston/Crazy motherfucker named Chase…"

They both laughed and kept walking.

"Hey, do you mind if I use your bathroom?" Chase asked. "I have to wicked piss."

"No problem," Michael said.

Suddenly Chase burst out laughing again.

Michael gave him a confused tilt of the head.

"I just noticed your shirt," Chase said.

Michael looked down. He'd forgotten what he was wearing, a t-shirt emblazoned with a rainbow-straddling unicorn and the words "Wish You Were Queer."

"Funny," Chase chuckled.

They arrived in the foyer of the pink, three story apartment house where Michael lived. Michael knew it was crazy to open his apartment to some punk kid he'd just met a few minutes ago. But, strangely, he didn't get that "I wonder if this guy is a serial killer" feeling that he sometimes experienced with even the most mild-mannered of dates. He also deeply wanted to know more about the guy.

Michael put his key in the lock. But before opening the door, he asked, "How old are you?"

Becoming a registered sex offender was not the kind of reinvention Michael was looking for."

"19," he said. "Just turned."

Michael opened the door and stepped into the living room. Some stray dust balls on the beige-tiled floor made Michael regret never un-boxing the Swiffer that he'd once bought on impulse at Target. He turned to close the door and led Chase into the bedroom, which you had to walk through in order to get to apartment's only bathroom.

Chase looked around at the bed and the desk with a 27" iMac on it.

"Fuck, that thing's huge," Chase said of the computer, "Must be great for watching porn."

Michael blushed. He hoped Chase hadn't noticed the small black trashcan underneath the desk. It was filled with so many balled-up tissues that it could've been used as a prop in a Claritin commercial.

"Over here," Michael said, pointing to the bathroom door.

While Chase was in the bathroom, Michael waited in the living room. He thought it was against some kind of etiquette to stand right outside the door while a stranger used your bathroom. Michael distractedly flipped through an issue of "Photo District News" until Chase walked back in the room.

"Hey, what's that?" Chase asked, pointing to a framed poster on the wall.

The picture was divided into three colored sections with stenciled words labeling the sections "blue," "yellow," and "red." Vertically stretched across the colors was a long black arm-print with fingers that splayed and reached toward the top of the frame.

"It's a poster by this artist I like, Jasper Johns," Michael said.

"It's cool," Chase said, moving toward it and peering at it closely. "I like the hand. It looks like it's reaching for the sky or something."

"It was inspired by this gay poet, Hart Crane," Michael explained. "He was talented, but never really got his due. And then one day, he jumped off the Brooklyn Bridge."

"See," Michael continued, pointing to the arm reaching out of the section marked 'Blue,' "that's supposed to be his hand sticking out of the water."

"Shit," Chase said. "What happened to him?"

"He drowned."

"That's fuckin' depressing." Chase said.

Michael shrugged. "Sometimes life sucks."

"Yeah," Chase said, backing away from the picture. Then he smiled. "But sometimes it doesn't."

Chase continued looking around the room, from the Ikea sofa, which had the crumbly consistency of stale toast, to the floor-to-ceiling bookshelves packed with thick art tomes. Chase studied the spines of the books that had boldfaced names like

Richard Avedon, Daido Moriyama, William Klein, Roy
DeCarava, Gordon Parks, and Jurgen Teller.

"Who are all these people?" Chase asked.

"Just photographers I like."

"You're a photographer?" Chase asked. "That's, like,
what you do?"

"Yep," Michael said.

"That's cool."

Michael nodded.

"Hey, do you think I could be a model?" Chase asked. "I
used to be a stripper down at XL."

Michael knew the place. It was the only gay strip club in
town. But as with most queer nudie bars from time immemorial,
the majority of the strippers were straight.

"People would always tell me that I could model," Chase
continued. "I mean, I knew that a lot of the guys just wanted me
to do porn and shit. But, you know, I still thought that maybe I
could one day model, like, legit."

"What kind of pictures would you want to take?"

"Like cool shit—"

Suddenly, the sounds of the Wu Tang Clan blasted through the room: "Cash rules everything around me/Cream, get the money/dollar-dollar-bill, y'all." Chase reached in his pocket and pulled out his phone. He glanced at the screen and grimaced.

"It's my girl," Chase said. "We're beefin'."

"So, he is straight," Michael thought. "Figures." He tried not to look disappointed.

Chase silenced the phone and placed it back in his pocket.

They were both quiet for a moment. Michael lowered his head and rubbed the back of his neck with his right hand. Chase continued perusing the bookshelf.

"Hey, you wanna get something to eat?" Michael asked.

"Sure," Chase said.

"Then, maybe we can come back here and take some pictures."

"Cool."

Michael took Chase to Tokyo, a Japanese restaurant on Wickenden. It was a low-key, almost dive-y BYOB place that was generally filled with Brown students and their paper bag-covered beers.

"Ever tried sushi?" Michael asked, when his spicy lobster roll arrived.

Chase, who'd ordered the chicken fried rice, shook his head.

"Dare you," Michael said, as he used his chopsticks to lift a piece of his roll and offer it to Chase. Chase leaned over, opened his mouth, and ate the sushi off of Michael's chopsticks. A few seconds later, a partially chewed piece of lobster roll dropped out of Chase's mouth and onto his plate of fried rice.

"Sorry, man," Chase said, wiping his lips with his napkin. "It's just not my thing."

Michael smiled. Then he realized he wasn't actually smiling at all; his mouth was full of lobster roll. It just *felt* like he was smiling.

After sushi, they stopped by Coldstone Creamery on Thayer. Michael ordered a cup of Sinless Sweet Cream; Chase got a large scoop of coffee ice cream with Oreos in a chocolate-dipped waffle cone. "It's cool what you do," Chase said, as they walked back to Michael's place.

"What's that?" Michael asked.

"You know, being a photographer and all. That's cool."

"Thanks."

"I wish I could be an artist and do my drawings and shit. Not just tag, you know?"

"So, do it."

"It's hard, man. I mean, I used to do it at school when I was younger. Won contests and shit. Was even up for a scholarship at RISD."

"What happened?"

"I fucked up. Dropped out. There was a lot goin' on."

He paused.

"But one day I'm gonna get my shit together," Chase said. "Get my G.E.D. Might even go to college."

"Good."

"That's my dream, at least. But who the fuck knows, you know?"

"Yeah," Michael said.

They continued walking down Thayer, past the Brown dorms. A curly-haired student in a Brown hoodie, khaki shorts, and flip-flops rolled by on his longboard. His oversized backpack brushed Michael's arm as he passed.

"How much you think it costs to go here?" Chase asked.

"Lots, I guess," said Michael.

Chase took the last bite from his cone and licked some ice cream drips from his thumb and forefinger.

"So, you still want to take pictures," Chase asked, once they were back at Michael's apartment.

Michael felt sluggish from the sushi/ice cream combo, but still said, "Yeah."

"I want you to make them wicked sexy," Chase said, stretching out on Michael's couch, "something for all my girls on the 'Gram."

Michael laughed. He walked into the small coat closet where he kept his equipment. He grabbed his Konica Big Mini.

"The only thing is," Michael said, "I don't do a lot of posed stuff. I like shit to look natural. So we have to think of a reason why you'd, you know, be looking sexy."

Chase thought for a moment. "How about we do something in the shower?"

"Uh, O.K.," Michael said, trying to hide his enthusiasm.

They entered the bathroom and Chase took off his clothes. *All* of his clothes. Michael had been prepared to ask if he'd feel more comfortable keeping his underwear on, but evidentially modesty wasn't an issue.

Chase stepped into the shower, and Michael noticed all of Chase's tattoos—a colorful array of crosses, skulls, and nautical stars. On his elbow was a heart with "Mom" written across it. On his torso was a beautiful blue bird soaring upward.

They took pictures for about 15 minutes. Michael was impressed with how Chase knew how to catch the light by angling his face and body just so. There was also a compelling intensity about his gaze. Chase was simply beautiful. Beautiful and sexy. Beautiful and sexy in a way that made Michael swell in his heart, as well as in other places. At one point, Michael had to take pictures from a squatted position in order to hide his erection.

Once they finished, Michael rose from the ground slowly and stiffly. He gave Chase a towel to dry off, then went to sit on the bed to rest his legs. He turned on the TV to catch the last few minutes of *All In with Chris Hayes*. Chase walked out of the bathroom, and Michael was surprised to see that he hadn't put his clothes back on. He was only wearing a towel wrapped around his waist.

"Can I ask you a question?" Chase said.

Michael pushed pause on the remote. "Sure."

"Would you mind if I crashed on your sofa tonight?"

The question made Michael freeze in mind and body.

"It's just that me and my girl are going at it. She don't want me to come home."

"You don't have anywhere else to go?" Michael said reflexively.

"Not really. Just my mom's. But me and her are sorta beefin' too. She thinks I smoke too much weed," Chase laughed.

Michael didn't say anything right away. He knew he shouldn't let the kid stay over. It was the sort of move that would make everyone tsk-tsk as they watched the reenactment of his murder on *Dateline*. But he really wanted more time with Chase. He really wanted him to stay.

"It's O.K. if you don't want me to," Chase said. "I mean, we just met. I probably shouldn't have asked."

"No, it's fine," Michael interrupted. He looked over at Chase, whose mouth curled into a grin.

They spent the rest of the evening watching TV on Michael's bed, close but not touching. Michael surrendered the remote to Chase, who chose to watch *Superbad*. "It was one of my favorite movies in junior high," Chase said, making Michael feel old enough to be encased in glass at the Natural History Museum.

When the movie was over, Chase said, "Guess I'll go to sleep now." He rose from the bed, opened his arms and wrapped Michael in a hug. "And really man, thanks for letting me stay."

"No problem," Michael said, hugging back tightly and hoping Chase couldn't feel his quickening heartbeat.

After Chase left the bedroom, Michael got ready for bed, brushing his teeth, and taking a piss. Then he searched in his drawers for a pair of pajama bottoms. He generally slept in the nude, but tonight, he thought it might be best to cover up.

Michael slipped into bed, but was unable to sleep. He kept feeling like he was close to sleep, but something stopped him from crossing over. It was precisely because he was in this weird state that he thought he was hallucinating when he heard a slight tapping at his door. But as the noise continued and steadily grew louder, he realized it was for real.

Then he heard his name.

"Michael?" Chase asked in a sleepy whisper.

"Yeah," Michael answered.

Chase entered the room.

"I know this is weird," he said, "but your couch is super-hard. I can't sleep. Do you mind if I stay in here?"

For the second time that night, Michael felt like he was smiling on the inside. He scooted over and patted the area next to him.

Chase got into the bed and moved back so that his body was just lightly touching Michael's.

"You can spoon me, but no dick up the ass," Chase said, laughing.

"Deal," Michael said, wrapping his arm snugly around Chase's hard, tight chest.

That was the beginning of...well, Michael never knew how to describe his relationship with Chase? Friends? Friends with benefits? Lovers? It depended on when the question was asked and how Michael chose to classify things. At some point, he stopped trying to explain the relationship to anyone including himself. It just was. And it changed everything about his life.

Creatively, it reinvigorated him. He photographed Chase all the time—walking through the city at night, posing against the backdrop of some fresh graffiti, dancing with girls at an underage nightclub, taking hits on his bong. Sidney saw some of the pictures and thought they were Michael's best work.

"Now *these* were worth moving for," Sidney said.

For a time, Michael's whole life seemed to be gelling, personally and professionally. Of course, Michael had been friendly with guys he'd photographed in the past. But before Chase, he'd never felt such a connection with any of his subjects. In fact, he'd never felt such a bond with anyone.

But the situation was far from ideal. There was rarely any tension between the two of them, but Chase would sometimes disappear for months at a time without any notice or contact. This generally meant that he had gotten back together with his girlfriend and was living somewhere in Massachusetts. Sometimes this was combined with Chase losing his cell phone or having it turned off for lack of payment. Once he was in jail for failing to appear in court on a minor traffic violation; another time he followed his friend's punk band down to Austin for SXSW.

These disappearances frustrated Michael, but he never let it show. He knew the last thing Chase wanted or needed was another person pressuring him. And the remarkable thing was that Chase always returned, sometimes calling, sometimes just showing up in Michael's foyer. Michael came to trust that Chase would eventually return no matter how long he was away.

But the last time Chase disappeared was different. They had made plans to meet one afternoon and Chase didn't show. Michael tried calling Chase's cell. There was no answer for the first couple of days; then he got an out-of-service message. Michael didn't know Chase's friends, so he couldn't ask them where he was. And he wasn't about to show up at Chase's mother's house in Cranston. How would that have played out?

He imagined a pretty blond woman, perhaps Michael's own age, answering the door. Michael would say: "Hello, I'm a nearly 40-year-old gay man who is in a pseudo-sexual relationship with your barley legal son. Is he in? Or do you know when you might be expecting him?"

It had now been more than a year since Michael last saw Chase. He'd worked his way through all of Kübler-Ross' stages of grief—denial, anger, bargaining, depression, and acceptance—which he knew these from repeated childhood viewings of *All That Jazz*. In many ways, his relationship with Jimmy had been a way to help him get over Chase. But ever since Jimmy broke up with him, Michael experienced that hollow sensation again, the one that came back with force whenever Chase was away.

"I love you," Michael said to the starless sky, as he continued walking to the Mirror Ball. It was something he often did, his way of letting Chase know that he was still there and he still cared.

Chapter 6

Michael walked into the Mirror Ball and headed for the upstairs bar. Since Sidney and Bruce weren't with him, he was hoping to spot some of his backup bar buddies like John, a copy editor at the *Providence Journal* or Terry, a professional party planner. Unfortunately, neither of them were there. It was probably one of Jim's late nights at the paper, and Terry was always flying to some convention or other, usually in Vegas.

Michael looked around. Seated by himself at the end of the bar was another regular, Tom. He was a big gray lump of a man, who worked at a nursing home in North Attleboro. There was an empty stool next to him, so Michael sat down.

"Hi there," Michael said.

Tom, who'd been staring into his drink, looked up with a start.

"Oh, hey," he said, patting Michael on the back and looking around the bar. "Where's your gang tonight?"

Michael turned his palms up. "They were all tired or had shit to do."

"Flying solo, huh?" Tom said, slurring his words slightly. Tom generally headed to the bar as soon as he got off from work in the afternoon and often stayed drinking until closing.

"Looks like it, yeah," Michael said.

Billy, one of the hunkier bartenders, walked over and smiled, flashing his white Chicklet teeth. "The usual?" he asked Michael.

"Yep," Michael said.

Billy nodded, smiled again, and went off to make the drink.

"So, it's just you tonight, huh?" Tom said. "The lone wolf."

"Yeah," replied Michael. "I just wanted to grab a drink and chill."

A couple of minutes passed in silence. Billy came back wnad placed Michael's drink in front of him.

Tom exhaled wheezily. "A man alone," Tom said, as if making a profound observation. "I guess…I guess we're two men alone tonight." He lifted his glass. "A toast to that."

Michael raised his drink and lightly tapped it against Tom's.

"It's a lonely fucking world out there, huh?" Tom said.

The relative loneliness of the world was the last thing Michael felt like discussing on a night when he was already down.

"You know," Michael said. "I once read this book where the writer wrote something like, 'It doesn't matter if you're actually alone or not; you're only truly lonely if you don't like who you're alone with.'"

"That's interesting," Tom said. "You know what I'd tell that writer?"

Michael shook his head.

"Fuck you," Tom said, raising his middle finger. He started to laugh, but the chuckles quickly turned into a microburst of dry, hoarse coughs. The coughing went on so long that the bartender came over and asked, "You O.K.?"

"Sure, I'm alright; I'm alright." Tom raised his glass. "I'll take another, though."

Michael took a big swallow of his drink. He wanted to finish quickly so he could move to another floor of the club, away from Tom.

"Whatever happened to that guy who you used to always be with, the young one?" Tom asked.

At first, Michael thought he was talking about Chase, but he couldn't recall ever bringing Chase here.

"You know, the one I'm talking about," Tom continued, "the Harry Potter-looking kid with the glasses. I see him at the Wal-Mart all the time."

"Oh, Jimmy," Michael said. "Um…well, we sorta broke up. It's a long story."

"That's too fucking bad," Tom said. He paused to sip some of his newly refreshed drink. "Well, you know what they say about life, don't ya? They say life is like—"

Michael stared at him quizzically as his mind ran through metaphors: a bowl of cherries, a box of chocolates...

Tom continued: "They say life is like a basketball game or a baseball game...any kind of ball game, really. Just a game in general, you know?"

Michael didn't, but nodded anyway.

"The point," Tom said, taking another sip, "the point is that life is like a game. Sometimes you find yourself winning; other times you're getting your fucking ass kicked. But the problem...the fucked up thing of it all is that you don't know how long the game will last. It's not like you're in it for 9 innings or 4 quarters or whatever..."

Tom belched abruptly before continuing: "See, if you're winning in any other game, you just have to hold out until the end and you know you'll be the winner. You just stay in the game until the clock runs out. But in life, in life you never know. Whether you're ultimately a winner or a loser all depends on when God blows the whistle. *That's* the fucked up thing about life. You never know when God is gonna blow the whistle."

Michael downed the rest of his drink and placed the glass on the bar.

"Um, I think I'm gonna walk around a little," Michael told Tom.

"Enjoy yourself," Tom said with a wave. "And watch out for that whistle."

Michael headed downstairs and tried to shake Tom's morbid thoughts from his mind. There wasn't much of a crowd, about a couple dozen people total. Some sat at the bar, a few danced listlessly on the dance floor. And there were assorted others standing along the dark walls.

Boring, Michael thought. He walked to the bar and decided to have one more drink before leaving.

It was as he was standing at the bar, sipping his drink, when he heard a voice behind him say, "Hey."

It wasn't a voice Michael recognized. He turned around and saw that it was the Mohawk Kid he'd spotted before.

"Hey," the guy repeated. "Will you hold my pants for me?"

"What?" Michael said.

"My pants, will you hold them for me?"

Michael looked down at the Mohawk Kid's legs, which were covered by a pair of low-riding skinny jeans.

"Aren't you, um, wearing them?" Michael said.

"Yeah, but I'm about to enter the underwear contest, and I really don't want to leave my pants in the back because people have gotten shit stolen."

"How do you know I'm not gonna steal your shit?"

"I've seen you around." The Mohawk Kid smiled. "You don't seem like the shit-stealing type."

"You've seen me around?" Michael said, surprised that he'd registered on the kid's radar.

"Dude, you're, like, here every night," the Mohawk Kid. Then he added, "I mean, no offense or anything,"

"None taken." Michael said. He felt his bad mood begin to makea shimmery dissolve, like a crewmember beaming from the Star Trek Enterprise.

"So, will you hold my pants?" the guy asked again.

"Sure," Michael said.

"Thanks. I'm gonna go take 'em off in the back."

The Mohawk Kid started walking away, but Michael stopped him.

"What's your name, by the way?" Michael asked. "I generally like to get a guy's name before I see him with his pants off."

"Man, you're old school," the kid laughed. "It's Ziggy. My mom was really into—"

"—morbidly obese cartoon characters," Michael joked.

"What?" Ziggy asked.

"Nothing."

"No, see, she was really into David Bowie. It was this whole thing."

"I had a friend in college who was really into Bowie," said Michael.

"Was he your boyfriend?" Ziggy asked.

"It was a she."

"Was she your girlfriend?"

94

"No, but we did sorta," Michael paused, thinking of the right word, "experiment."

"Well, what's your name?" Ziggy asked.

"Michael. My mom was really into the Jackson 5."

"Seriously?"

"No," Michael said, laughing out loud for the first time that night. "You're pretty gullible for a guy with spikes coming out of his head."

Ziggy mouthed "whatever" and walked away. Michael took a sip from his glass. He was shocked to find that it was almost empty.

About five minutes later, the contestants in the underwear contest made their way out of a small door with an "Employees Only" sign on it. First, there was Ziggy, clad in a tight pair of black briefs that were covered with tiny skulls. He smiled at Michael and handed him the jeans.

Michael couldn't help but notice Ziggy's lean, tan body. "I used to look like that," Michael thought and resolved to start running again.

Michael didn't recognize the next guy to come out. He was a small, muscular Latino guy with a gigantic star tattoo on the right side of his neck. Next came Bruce's former hookup Nutz. His package, wrapped tightly in a pair of plaid briefs, looked like something you might put on a picnic table as a centerpiece.

Following Nutz was a baseball-cap-wearing guy in saggy nondescript boxers. Michael figured he must have been a last minute addition. The guy's wobbly gait suggested that booze had something to do with the decision.

Behind this guy was a familiar, bespectacled face, Michael's ex, Jimmy in a pair of Spiderman boxer briefs. It surprised Michael to see Jimmy in the contest. He'd always been self-conscious about his body when they dated.

"Uh, hey," Michael said, as Jimmy passed by.

"Hey," Jimmy replied, not making eye contact.

"Didn't expect to see you in the contest."

"Yeah, well," Jimmy said, looking down and adjusting his waistband.

As Jimmy spoke, Michael realized that he'd become very drunk from the combination of back-to-back drinks and no food since the sweaty cheese tray that he'd eaten on the train from Manhattan. Michael looked over at Jimmy's body. It seemed firmer somehow, like he'd been working out. "I guess, what I meant to say is..." Michael continued. "I guess...you look really good."

"You *guess* I look really good? Gee, thanks, Michael!" Jimmy said as walked away, shaking his head.

"No, I mean..." But before Michael could finish, Jimmy was already following the rest of the contestants assembled in front of the stage, where a tall, drag queen in an electric blue mini-dress stood holding a glitter-covered microphone.

"Hello, ladies and ladies," the queen said to the all-male crowd "Welcome to the Mirror Ball's monthly underwear contest. *I'm* Monica Brandy, and *you* need to give it up. The boy is mine."

A ripple of laughter ran through the crowd, even though most of the people had heard the line many times before.

"Now, how are you horny motherfuckers tonight?" Monica asked. "Are you ready for some hot-ass boys?"

"Yeah," several guys yelled. There were even a couple of "hell yeah"-s and at least one "fuck yeah."

"I swear," Monica said, "it's like *Providence's Next Top Twink* in this motherfucker tonight. I've got some young ones for you. Is that alright?"

"Yeah!" Michael drunkenly shouted, sooner and louder than anyone else. A couple of heads turned his way.

"As Tyra Banks once said…" Monica dramatically lowered her voice. "You know our prizes."

The crowd laughed.

"No, seriously, first place tonight is $100. And that's cash. You don't want to take a check from here, not in this motherfuckin' economy. Our money is too funny. We got Fred Sanford money. J.J. Evans money. Dorothy, Rose, Blanche, *and* Sophia money. You feel me? Our money got jokes for days."

More laughter from the crowd.

"But, anyway, that's first place, $100." Monica turned to the contestants. "And Lord knows, many of ya'll up have given up ass for less. Now, the second place winner gets a $50 bar tab. And the third place winner gets a free blow job in the bathroom from that guy over there."

Monica pointed to a random guy in a red t-shirt who was on his phone. He looked up as if he'd been caught in a firing squad.

"No, chile, you can relax," Monica said to him. "The third place winner gets a $25 bar tab, but you can still suck him off if you want to."

The guy's face was now the color of his shirt.

"Well, let's get started," Monica said. "I'm gonna bring the contestants up here one by one. And when we're done with the introductions, I want you to applaud for your favorite, O.K.?"

Someone in the crowd started clapping.

"Not yet, bitch," Monica snapped. She looked at a piece of paper in her hand. "Now, first up is a young cutie named Ziggy. Come on up, baby."

Ziggy climbed up on stage with his back to the audience. He gave his ass a few shakes, and some guys hooted.

"Now, Ziggy, how old are you?"

"19," Ziggy said. He held up his the backs of his hands, which had two black magic marker Xs on them. The doorman drew Xs on the hands of anyone under 21.

"Jesus, Lord, 19," said Monica. "Do you even any hair down there?"

Ziggy grinned, pulled open the waistband of his briefs, and motioned for Monica to look down. Monica opened the waistband, leaned over and took a long peek.

"Gentlemen," she announced in a stately manner. "I can confirm a bush."

More whoops from the crowd.

"Now give us a little dance so we can see what you're working with."

The DJ threw on Nicki Minaj's "Anaconda." Ziggy stomped around the stage for a couple of minutes, grabbing his crotch and making heavy metal devil signs with his hands. Then he turned around, bent over and shook his butt some more. The crowd roared appreciatively.

When Ziggy was done, Monica pointed for Nutz to come onstage.

"Our next contestant is Jordan," Monica said.

"So that's Nutz's real name," Michael thought.

"And how old are you, Jordan?" Monica asked.

"21. Just turned," he answered.

"I told y'all we have some young ones tonight," Monica said. "Now let's see you move a little."

The DJ started the music again and Nutz wildly thrust his crotch to the beat. After a few moments, Monica interrupted.

"Wait a minute," Monica said. "Wait a Goddamn minute. DJ, stop the music, please."

Monica stared at Nutz's enormous bulge and asked, "Boy, what in the hell have you got in your pants?"

Nutz stood proudly with his hands on his hips.

"Those nuts look like tennis balls," Monica continued. "It's like motherfuckin' Wimbledon down there."

Monica took her hand and cupped his package. "I have never felt such big-ass balls in all my natural born life. I'd be scared as a motherfucker to suck that dick. One of them wrecking balls could hit you in the face and break your motherfuckin' jaw. I don't have enough Obamacare for that dick."

The crowd laughed and Nutz blushed.

Next up was the Latino guy that Michael didn't recognize. Guys came from all parts of New England to participate in the contest since it was a good way to make quick money.

"This is Diego, everybody," Monica said. "And how old are you, Papi?"

"24"

"24? Aw, shucks, he's the daddy of the group, y'all."

Diego did a quick spin and a little salsa two-step. The crowd cheered again.

"Our last contestant is a guy you're probably used to seeing around here. It's our own glasses-wearing cutie, Jimmy. Come on up, baby."

Jimmy took the stage with his eyes looking down and his hands across his thin freckled chest.

"And look," Monica said, pointing into the audience, "that's his boyfriend, Michael, right there. Here to support your man? I know that's right."

Jimmy whispered something into Monica's ear. Monica made a pearl-clutching gesture.

"Oh, I'm sorry, folks," Monica said. "Looks like I have to issue a retraction. Our little Jimmy and Michael are apparently no longer together."

Several guys went "awwww."

"Yeah, that's very sad," Monica said. "It's always sad when people breakup. But, on the bright side, they'll both be available for rebound sex immediately following our program."

Michael stared at his shoes.

"So, Jimmy, how old are you now?"

"23"

"23 and oh so sweet. Do a little turnaround for us, baby."

Jimmy did a slow, circular shuffle, then returned to standing in place with his arms across his chest.

"Now, the winner is based on audience applause," Monica explained. "So if you like somebody, don't hang back and be cool, you need to clap. Are ya'll with me?"

"Yeah!" rang the crowd.

"First, let's hear it for our little 19-year-old Ziggy. If you like your guys young with freshly sprouted pubes, put your hands together."

Ziggy pulled his underwear down in the front so that you could see a tuft of wiry black hair peeking out over the waistband. The crowd's cheers grew appreciatively louder.

"Y'all are some dirty ass old men," Monica said.

She then solicited claps for Nutz. " Now who wants to suck these jawbreaker balls?" she asked.

Nutz didn't get as loud a response as Ziggy, but there were at least a few vocal testicle enthusiasts.

Lastly, she called the names of Diego and Jimmy.

During this whole process, Michael was torn about his votes. Jimmy was his ex-boyfriend, but he was holding Ziggy's pants. In the end, he chose to give Jimmy and Ziggy the same number of claps, 10, delivered with equal intensity.

Unfortunately, that wasn't enough to save Jimmy who was dismissed after the first round. Next to go was Nutz. The final bout was between Ziggy and Diego. The applause that each contestant generated was so close that Monica had to ask the audience to vote again.

"O.K., people," Monica said, "I want you to *only* vote for the guy you want to win. If I see one of you motherfuckers voting twice, I'm gonna clock you upside the head with one of my Faux-boutins. Are we clear? Now, who wants Diego?"

Diego flexed his pecs and pumped his fists in the air to a barrage of loud cheers, hoots, and hollers.

"What about our youngin' Ziggy?" Monica asked.

Ziggy walked to the edge of the stage, cupped his left hand around his dick and balls, and used his right hand to pull down his briefs. He stepped out of his underwear and jumped up and down, spinning his briefs around with his free hand. The audience responded with a noise that couldn't have been louder if Ziggy had been the tyrannical dictator of a tiny, twink nation.

"I think we have our winner," Monica said.

Ziggy did a bare ass victory lap and then jumped offstage headed toward Michael. As Michael unfolded the pants to hand back to Ziggy, he felt a vibration. All of a sudden, a glowing, buzzing iPhone fell out from one of Ziggy's pockets. Michael reached down and grasped it just before it hit the ground.

He looked at the phone.

"Apparently, there's a 'Mom' calling for you," Michael said to Ziggy.

Ziggy took the phone and silenced it.

"So, can I have my pants back now? My ass cheeks are getting cold."

"Are you sure you're done flashing people for the night?"

"Unless you want a private show later," Ziggy said.

Michael blushed. "I can't tell if you're serious or not."

"Why don't you try to figure it out while I put my pants on," Ziggy said.

Michael handed him the jeans and Ziggy walked away. Just before he entered the "Employee's Only" door, Ziggy glanced back toward Michael, bent over and gave his naked ass another shake. Michael shook his head and smiled.

Once Ziggy disappeared behind the door, Michael headed back upstairs. He didn't want to wait right by the door like some stalker. "Best play it cool," Michael thought.

The upstairs bar had emptied considerably. Tom was still there, again quietly staring into his drink. Michael didn't want to get into another conversation with him so he sat at the other end of the bar in front of a video game where you looked at two nearly identical pictures of scantily clad guys and pointed out the slight differences between them. Michael stuck a dollar in the slot and started playing.

As Michael selected various misaligned pecs, biceps, and abs, he thought about how much better he now felt from earlier in the evening. Just meeting Ziggy had given Michael a boost. It was a reminder that you never really knew when someone new was going to come into your life.

Michael pulled his phone out of his pocket and checked the time. About fifteen minutes had passed since he left Ziggy. He decided to go back downstairs and look for him. But as he reached the second floor landing, he noticed Monica Brandy staring out of the large window that looked onto the street. Michael moved closer to see what she was looking at. It was Diego, the Latino guy who finished second place, making out with another guy underneath a streetlight. That other guy was Ziggy.

"Some consolation prize, huh?" Monica asked.

But Michael was already on his way back down the stairs. It seemed that his luck hadn't changed after all. He walked out of the club and texted Bruce: "911."

Part Three

Chapter 7

Michael awoke the next morning and realized he wasn't home. This was clear as soon as he opened his eyes and saw the wall across from him—hospital white and bare except for a framed poster of a red Ferrari. Directly in front of the wall was a black metal chair with a thick blue jacket hanging on the back of it. At its base were two black lace-up boots. Michael knew, in that instant, whose house this was and whose arm was lightly curled around him. Both belonged to Bruce.

Michael closed his eyes again and hazily pieced together the events that had gotten him here. He'd been about to leave the Mirror Ball when he sent Bruce the text "911." It was a code they'd come up with early in their friendship. When they first met at the Mirror Ball, Michael was in one of those periods when he didn't know where Chase was or how to contact him. Bruce, at the time, was between boy toys. Michael and Bruce bonded mostly over their mutual appreciation for twinks. But there was also a Paula Abdul/MC Skat Kat opposites-attract vibe between them; the artsy photographer guy meets the butch cop. They hooked up a few times right off the bat, and while the sex was enjoyable, it was never quite right. Bruce insisted on being the top, and Michael was a rather begrudging bottom. Neither had much stamina for cocksucking, and Bruce was grossed out by rimming—one of Michael's favorite things to do and have done to him.

Michael and Bruce knew that the sex could be better if they practiced at it. But neither wanted to do the work it would take for them to become sexually compatible. They also weren't really sure if a romantic relationship was what they really wanted with each other, anyway. Some of their most enjoyable times were at the Mirror Ball debating the relative hotness of *other* guys. Eventually Michael and Bruce chose to stop having sex in order to preserve something that, in the context of their lives, seemed more precious: friendship.

But they also had an understanding that if they ever needed each other in a sexual way, if in any given moment, one of them wanted a familiar touch and not the arms, dick or ass of a stranger, they could text "911." It seemed like the perfect plan. They were friends and "in case of emergency" fuck buddies.

This system's launch was a little rocky. Initially, Michael thought that Bruce was abusing the plan by using "911" every time some twink didn't immediately return a text. But this got sorted out after a few stern talks. Shortly thereafter, Michael started seeing Jimmy, and the arrangement was put on hold whenever one of them was dating someone exclusively. Last night marked the first time either one of them had used the code in more than a year. It felt nice.

As Michael lay under Bruce's thick, muscled arm, he wondered if maybe they should give the relationship thing another go. Would it be worth risking their friendship? Were things different enough for it to work now? Both of them still preferred twinks, but that attraction—or, as Sidney would put it, "crippling obsession"—didn't seem to be making either of them happy.

Michael couldn't seem to find a guy who wanted the same things he wanted. Most of the younger guys he talked to either wanted to avoid commitment altogether or jump straight to the wedding ceremony. Michael understood what drove these commitment crazies. There are so few certainties in your 20s that it felt calming to have at least one big life decision settled. But Michael was old enough to know that anything that felt like certainty was probably an illusion. He didn't want to toke on anyone else's pipe dream. The only relationship Michael could believe in was one that took things day-by-day.

The problem with his relationship with Jimmy was that Michael thought it was rushing things to move in together. Michael didn't want to live with anyone at this point. He had too much stuff to focus on. There were still too many things that he wanted to accomplish in life. He needed the space to be selfish and not have someone around all the time, wanting and needing things from him. He loved the time he spent with Jimmy, but he had also liked that Jimmy could go home.

Michael knew that living together wouldn't be an issue if he dated Bruce. If anyone appreciated space, it was Bruce. Maybe if he and Bruce started dating, they could give each other some purpose. Maybe this time it could work.

Lying there in bed, Michael liked the feel of Bruce's big tree branch of an arm around him. He'd liked the sex too. It was better than it had been before. Everything flowed better. When Bruce fucked him, Michael actually enjoyed it. He didn't want it to go on forever, mind you. But it was fine while it lasted.

Michael wondered if potential happiness was right in front of him, or, rather, sleeping behind him. His mind was in the midst of conjuring a multitude of romantic scenarios—snowy weekend getaways, island vacations—when Bruce shifted slightly in his sleep. Michael felt Bruce lift his right leg slightly. Then he unleashed a long, thunderous fart—the sound and smell of which snapped Michael back to reality. He slipped out of bed, careful not to wake Bruce, gathered his clothes and quietly headed home.

#

Less than a mile away, in a dorm room at the Rhode Island School of Art and Design, Ziggy's iPhone vibrated on his nightstand. It was his mother.

"This is *so* not regulation," Ziggy answered, laying back on his bed.

"What?" Traci asked.

"This call," Ziggy said. "It's so off the books."

"What are you talking about."

"Remember, we agreed, no phone calls before 10."

"It's a quarter 'til."

"That wouldn't stand up in court." Ziggy said.

"Besides, I didn't expect you to answer," Traci said.

"Then why'd you call?" Ziggy asked, sitting up.

"I was worried. I called last night and you didn't answer and you didn't text"

"I know," Ziggy said. "I was at a club. It was totally embarrassing. Some guy was holding my phone when you called."

"Why was he holding your phone?" Traci asked.

"Because he was holding my pants." Ziggy explained.

"Why was he holding your pants?"

"It's a really long story." Ziggy sighed.

"I have time."

"Well, I don't. I have class in half an hour." He paused. "Or I could tell you the whole story, but then I'd have to skip class."

"You are ridiculous."

"Hold on for a moment," Ziggy said. Diego from the previous night's underwear contest walked in the room. He'd stayed over at Ziggy's and was returning from the bathroom.

"So, you found it O.K.?" Ziggy asked him.

"Who are you talking to?" Traci asked.

"What was your name again?" Ziggy asked the shirtless man in front of him.

"Diego," the guy said, scratching his balls.

"Diego," Ziggy said into the phone.

"Who is he?" Traci asked.

"Kind of a new friend," Ziggy said. He smiled at Diego and grasped one of his hands.

"The guy who was holding your pants?" Traci asked.

"No, that was a different guy."

Diego moved behind Ziggy on the twin bed and softly kissed his neck.

"Look, mom, I should probably…"

Diego kisses grew faster and he began circling Ziggy's nipples with his fingers.

"Um, I gotta call you back," Ziggy said to his mother, before quickly disconnecting.

He turned toward Diego, who wrapped his arms around Ziggy's thin waist.

"That was your mom?" Diego asked.

"Yeah," Ziggy said, burying his face in the crook of Diego's neck.

"You guy's close?" Diego asked, again running his fingers in circles around Ziggy's now-pointed nipples.

"You could say that," Ziggy said, almost whispering into Diego's ear.

"You close to your dad too?"

Ziggy shook his head. "You couldn't really say *that*."

"What happened?" Diego asked, his fingers briefly stopping their dance on Ziggy's chest.

Ziggy fell back on the bed. "It's kind of a long story and I have class in half an hour. So either I tell you all about my daddy issues or you can fuck me one more time?"

Diego flipped Ziggy onto his stomach and grabbed a condom from the nightstand.

Chapter 8

About a week later, Bruce was at the Mirror Ball in the middle of telling a story: "So, I put his hands in the cuffs and I'm fucking him, right? I'm lying on my back and he's facing me and riding me. He's a skinny twink, but he's got this big ol' bubble butt. I'm sorta spreading his ass cheeks apart so I can get in good. And I keep noticing that he's turning his head around a lot. I realize that he's watching himself get fucked in the mirror on my dresser. It was my grandparents' mirror, funny enough. Their dresser too, now that I think about it. But anyway, this kid is totally getting off on watching himself get fucked, and I'm getting off on the fact that he's getting off. This goes on for a while. And he's totally pumping his ass up and down, faster and faster. So, at this point, I'm like, fuck it, I'm gonna shoot my load. I pull out, take the rubber off my dick, toss it toward the trashcan and totally make the shot. I feel like a fucking rock star. I give my dick a couple of yanks and nut all over the twink's ass cheeks. But now here's where things get interesting…"

Bruce, Michael and Sidney were sitting at a small table on the top floor. It had been a couple of weeks since they'd seen each other. Bruce was catching them up on his latest sex-ploits. Michael was glad to hear Bruce talk about sex with another guy because it meant—at least, he hoped it meant—that there was no lingering weirdness from their hookup.

Bruce continued: "So, the guy tells me that he once saw this porno where a dude gets fucked with a nightstick. These kids, I'm tellin' ya, they're obsessed with porn. Been watching it their whole lives on their phones and shit. You know how we were, like, Generation X? They're, like, Generation Sex. So, anyway, he wants me to stick my nightstick up his butt while he watches in the mirror. Once guys know I'm a cop, they ask to do some crazy shit like suck on my gun and shit like that. But normally I stop at just using my cuffs. This guy was so fucking hot, though. And he had his ass cheeks spread open, like his lil' asshole was just begging for it—"

Bruce's phone, which sat on the table, lit up and started playing Guns n Roses' "Paradise City." Bruce glanced at the keypad and told his friends to hold on for a minute.

"Hello…No problem…What?… Oh, crap!…No, thanks, thanks for calling…I'll be right there." Bruce spoke into the phone.

"I gotta run," he said to Michael and Sidney.

"You didn't leave some twink cuffed to your bed again?" Michael asked.

"No," Bruce said. "And, for the record, that wasn't my fucking fault. That nutcase cuffed himself to the bed *after* I left for work."

"So what's up?" Michael asked.

"Nothing. Just got some shit I got to take care of."

"You can tell us about sticking a nightstick up some twink's ass, but you can't tell us where you're going?" Michael said.

"Gotta run," Bruce said, kissing Michael on the top of the head before rushing out of the bar.

"What do you think that's about?" Michael asked Sidney.

"God only knows," Sidney said with a shrug.

"What could he possibly have to do that he couldn't tell us about?"

"Everybody has secrets." Sidney said.

"I don't."

"Oh, you have them," Sidney said. "And you're no good at keeping them either."

"What do you mean?"

"Like the fact that you and Bruce slept together again." Sidney made a Dr. Evil-like grin and placed his pinky on his lips.

"How'd you know?" Michael said, mildly startled.

"For one, you just admitted it," Sidney said, sipping his Old Fashioned like it was a cup of tea.

"You're an asshole."

"There's always this thing between you two, and sometimes it seems stronger than others—"

"You're psychic now?"

"No, just a keen observer of the obvious."

"You really sense something between us?" Michael asked.

"Why? Do you have feelings for him?"

"Not like that." Michael shook his head.

"So why'd you guys hook up again?"

"I was having a bad night," Michael sighed. He took a gulp from his drink and tried to change the subject. "But enough about me. What's up with you lately? You haven't been around much."

"Work, just work," Sidney said. "This might come as a surprise, but your photos don't exactly sell themselves."

"Fuck you!" Michael said.

"Sorry, it's been a long—" Sidney started to say "day." "It's been a long *everything*."

"Well, make it up to me by buying me another drink."

Sidney handed Michael a $20 bill.

"You want something?" Michael asked.

"No, still working on this," Sidney said, holding up a half-full glass of brown liquid.

Michael nodded and headed to the bar.

Sidney realized he was on edge, but it had nothing to do with work and everything to do with Dante. He didn't want Michael to find out how much he'd been seeing Dante lately. He wasn't ready to be the cliché middle-aged queen who falls for a hustler. The whole point of using escorts was so that he wouldn't fall for anyone. But this thing with Dante was taking an entirely different course.

Sidney had been seeing Dante at least once a week for well over a month now. The frequency was deliberate. Sidney didn't want to see Dante more times than he was willing to pay for, even though Dante kept insinuating that he would spend time with Sidney for free. Sidney just couldn't believe this was true. Perhaps it was a weird marketing ploy: convince a guy that you'd see him for free so that he becomes emotionally invested and is then willing to pay more. They don't call it hustling for nothing.

But Dante, unlike a lot of escorts Sidney had met, didn't strike him as especially duplicitous or conniving. Maybe he was just really good at playing the game.

One night in bed, Dante was riding Sidney's cock so hard that it made Sidney recall a *Dr. Oz* episode on which Oz explained that it was actually possible to break your penis. To avoid injury, Sidney ordered Dante on his back, and not long afterward, they both came, creating a creamy pool on Dante's rippled stomach.

"We should do this more," Dante said, his voice scratchy and spent. "Like every night. Like a couple of times a night."

Sidney stayed silent.

"I told you, you don't have to pay any more," Dante said, reaching for Sidney's hand.

"Why?" Sidney asked, moving his hand away and reaching for his t-shirt at the end of the bed. Post-coital nudity made him uncomfortable.

"'Cause I like you." Dante said.

"You have a thing for old Negroes with money?"

"It ain't even like that."

"Then what is it like?"

"I mean, you've done something with your life, something interesting. You're not just some basic-ass, 9 to 5 nigga. You own your own shit. You're a boss. I like that."

Sidney didn't respond. It was always interesting to hear how you're perceived by others.

Dante continued: "Plus we talk about real shit."

"You don't talk to your other…" Sidney wasn't sure of the right word to use; "customers" seemed too retail-y. "…clients?"

"Not really," Dante said. "They usually just want to live out some thug fantasy and too much talk breaks the mood. Besides, most of them don't have shit to say anyway. They're just living life, going through the motions. But not you. You made the life you wanted. I want to be like that."

Dante sat up and used a wet wipe to swab the cum from his stomach. "I'm probably not even gonna do this much longer."

"Escorting?" Sidney asked with more urgency than he'd intended.

"Yeah," Dante said. "I'm kinda over it."

"What changed?"

"Don't know. I just feel different now."

They sat on the bed in silence for a few moments. There were so many follow-up questions that Sidney wanted to ask, but he feared that each question would lead him deeper into a place where he wasn't prepared to go.

As Sidney waited for Michael to return to the table, he got out his phone to browse the *New York Times* arts headlines. He was reading about an upcoming Albert Watson retrospective, when a notification appeared on the screen. It was a text from Dante: "Can I see you?"

Sidney had already seen him once this week, but before his brain could weigh the decision, he typed: "Yes."

Michael got back to the table, drink in hand.

"Wanna go downstairs and dance?" Michael asked.

"Actually, I think I'm gonna head out," Sidney answered.

"Now? Why?"

"Because I'm a grown-ass man and I can do what I want," Sidney said impatiently.

"Whatever," Michael said rolling his eyes.

Michael gave Sidney a quick goodbye hug and headed downstairs. As soon as he stepped on the dancefloor, something or someone crashed against him. It was Ziggy thrashing around as if he were in a mosh pit.

"Ow," Michael said.

"My bad," said Ziggy. He was shirtless and his body shone with sweat.

"Thanks for holding my pants the other night." Ziggy said.

"What?" Michael yelled over the music.

"My pants! Thanks for holding them the other night," Ziggy yelled directly into Michael's ear.

"No worries." Michael tried to give the impression that holding a random guy's pants was such a regular occurrence for him that Ziggy's held no special significance.

"Hey, come talk to me," Ziggy said. He took Michael's hand and dragged him off the dancefloor.

"What about?" Michael asked, reluctantly following.

"I was wondering if you wanted to hold my pants again, maybe at your place?"

"I'll pass." Michael said, still smarting from the night Ziggy hooked up with the Latino guy instead of him. He started to walk away.

Ziggy reached out and grabbed Michael's arm. "What's your problem? I thought we were cool."

Michael didn't really want to say anything, but he found himself blurting out: "Where's your boyfriend from the other night?"

"What boyfriend?" Ziggy asked.

"The guy you left with after the contest."

"He's not my boyfriend. We just hooked up that night. He doesn't even live around here."

Michael shrugged.

"I came out looking for you, but I didn't see you," Ziggy said. "Then that guy started talking to me. He needed a place to crash. And, you know, one thing led to another..."

"It's no big deal," Michael said. "Why are you even telling me all this?"

"'Cause I like you," Ziggy said. "You seem fun or at least you did the other night."

Ziggy hopped up on a carpeted platform near the dancefloor and sat down. He patted the spot next to him to suggest Michael do the same.

Michael sat down. "O.K., I admit I was a little pissed because you told me to wait for you and the next thing I know, you're outside tonguing down the Latino guy."

"Was just bad timing, dude. And, of course, we can make up for lost time." Ziggy touched Michael's hand.

Michael blushed. "I'm old enough to be your, I don't know, sperm donor."

After all of the younger guys he's dated, Michael still found himself saying these type of clichés and then immediately regretting it.

"I dig older guys sometimes," Ziggy said. "Less drama." Then he paused and looked at Michael: "Well, usually."

Michael laughed. "You have some daddy issues to work through or something?"

"Not really because I don't really have one."

"What?" Michael asked.

"A dad," Ziggy said.

Michael thought about saying, "I'm sorry." But he figured that would be patronizing.

"I am the result of modern science," Ziggy explained.

"Test tube baby?"

"The preferred term is donor-conceived-person," Ziggy said.

Michael wasn't sure what to say. He didn't know if donor-conception was on the rapidly expanding list of things that people had to be hyper-p.c. about. "That's interesting." Michael said.

"No, actually, it's kinda boring." Ziggy jumped to his feet. "So, are we hooking up or what?"

"Tempting," Michael said. "But I don't really hook up that much."

"What do you mean?"

"What do you mean, 'What do I mean?' I don't really hook up. Well, I usually don't. Every now and then I'll get super horny and, you know, something might go down. Something probably would have gone down on underwear night. But generally, I like to get to know a guy a little bit before introducing him to my junk."

"Wow, you're old school," said Ziggy. "Do you, like, believe in love and shit?"

"Of course, I believe in love," Michael said. "You don't?"

"I used to believe," Ziggy said. "Sometimes I still want to believe. I guess, for me, love is a lot like a Sasquatch."

Michael laughed.

"Well, are you gonna ask me out on a date or something?" said Ziggy.

"I don't even know if I want to date you," Michael said.

Both of them were silent for a few moments.

"But would you go?" Michael asked.

Maybe." Ziggy said, twisting his mouth contemplatively.
"Give me your number and I'll think about it."

When Michael got home later that night, he received a
text message with a photo. The picture was of Ziggy with the
word "Yes" written in black magic marker across his chest.

Chapter 9

A few days after abruptly rushing out of the Mirror Ball,
Bruce was scrubbing thick, mounds of burnt tomato sauce from
his kitchen stove. It was tedious because he was trying not to
scratch the vintage white enamel. It took his every ounce of
resolve not to rip the stovetop off and toss it in the middle of the
street. But he knew he had to keep cool. He'd never imagined
that he'd become one of those people who had to worry about
losing his temper, who had to try to say the right things in the
right non-threatening tone. He thought he'd gotten a pass
because he never had kids. But life was a tricky fucker.

Bruce finished with the stove, opened the refrigerator and grabbed a Bud Light. He swallowed nearly half of it in one gulp. He then walked into the living room, dropped heavily onto the sofa, and took a deep breath. A mix of burnt tomatoes and Formula 409 filled his nostrils. For some reason, the smell made him want to cry. But he took another pull from his beer and the feeling passed.

Bruce grabbed the TV remote from an end table and inadvertently knocked over a small picture frame. He caught it just before it hit the floor. It was a picture of his mother taken in the '70s when Bruce was a baby. The photo had been on the table since Bruce found it in a box of miscellaneous family stuff when cleaning up his basement. Bruce wondered at the time where to put it. He certainly didn't want it in the bedroom. It was kind of a mood killer to see your mother's face while you're fucking. So he randomly placed it on this table and never gave it any more thought.

The way he dealt with the photo was similar to the way he generally handled his mother. He never really gave much thought to her life, even after his father died several years ago.

He'd call his mother a couple of times a month at her home in Florida, where his parents moved after retiring. He was always relieved, when the answer to his question, "How are you, Ma?" was a plain spoken, "Fine."

Things were different now, though. His mother was demanding more and more from him, taking up more space in his life. It almost felt like revenge.

Bruce first noticed that something had changed when he visited his mom around Christmastime. As he walked through the flat, one-story house, he started noticing empty spaces where things had always been. For instance, there was just a shiny ring on the dining room table where a large fruit bowl once sat.

"Ma, what happened to the bowl?" Bruce asked. He had a taste for a Granny Smith apple.

"Bowl?" she answered. "What bowl?"

"The bowl with the fruit, the bowl that's *always* here."

"A bowl? Oh, I don't know."

Bruce starred at her, confused.

"Every time I turn around, something's gone," she added.

Bruce rubbed his temples.

"Are you ready for some breakfast?" his mother asked.

Bruce shook his head. It was 8:43 p.m.

Later that night, after his mother went to sleep, Bruce
made a list of all of the things that were missing from the house.
There was one of his father's bowling trophies, an abstract
painting that had been done by a family friend, all but one of the
televisions, and, most disturbingly, his mother's Yorkie, Jack.
Bruce never liked the yippy dog, so it had taken him a while to
notice he wasn't there.

"Liver cancer," his mother explained the next morning.
"Didn't I tell you?"

Bruce shook his head.

"Well, you never asked."

His mother was less clear about the other missing stuff,
snapping at him that she couldn't be bothered to remember every
little thing. Bruce was looking around the garage, when he
discovered a shoebox full of receipts from a place called "PAWS

FOR LIFE." It turned out to be the name of a local no-kill animal shelter that was partially funded by a charity thrift shop.

"Oh, yeah, she's one of our best donators," said the guy on the phone when Bruce called. "Every time we make the rounds, she gives us something good."

"You didn't think it was weird, her giving away all her stuff?" Bruce said, irritated.

"She kept saying she wanted to downsize, that she had too much junk, that there was no one in house but her," the man on the phone said. "I don't know. My personal opinion is that she was pretty broken up after her cat died. Wanted to do something for other animals."

"It was a dog," said Bruce.

"Oh right, the dog."

Bruce thanked the man for his information, but told him sternly not to accept any more donations from his mother. He then said something to the stranger that he had yet to admit to himself. "I'm not sure everything is alright with her."

The next week passed in a flurry of doctor's appointments and diagnoses. Alzheimer's disease is what the doctor said. Bruce wondered why he added disease to the end of it. Everybody knew what it was, what it meant.

"Can she still live alone?" Bruce asked the doctor privately.

"Can she?" said the doctor. "Yes. Should she? I'd say, probably not. You never know when these things will take a turn. It's good, critical sometimes, to have a loved one nearby to monitor the situation."

Bruce didn't respond right away. But after a few seconds, he offered his hand to the doctor and said, "thanks." He decided in that moment to ask his mother to move in with him. His house had a spare apartment with a separate entrance that he usually rented out to college kids. The place was pretty private. The only thing they had to share was the kitchen.

Bruce wasn't sure how long the arrangement would last. He didn't even know if he would be able to care for his mother if things got bad and messy. But for now, having her live with him seemed like the right thing to do, or perhaps it was more like, every other option seemed very wrong. His mother was initially resistant to the idea, almost as if for show, Bruce thought. But ultimately she said yes.

The plan worked well, initially. His mother seemed renewed, almost as if she were on vacation. Then after several happily uneventful weeks, things worsened. There was the time she took Bruce's car keys while he was sleeping. She drove God knows where, and then parked his truck in the driveway of a house three blocks away. This was the beginning of the wandering spells. Pretty soon, he was getting calls from neighbors about finding her in a nightgown, walking in the middle of the street.

One night, he was out with Michael and Sidney when a police buddy called. The officer had been patrolling Bruce's neighborhood when he noticed that the front door to Bruce's house was open. Bruce rushed home and couldn't find his mother anywhere. He was worried because, although the neighborhood was mostly safe, it had its share of crime. He walked all the side streets near his house for about an hour searching for her. Then he jumped in his truck and methodically drove up and down Wickenden. He finally found her about an hour later sitting on a bench by the river downtown. He figured that she had just kept walking down the street until she reached the water.

Bruce jumped out of the car and went over to her. She was dressed in a bright t-shirt, a straw hat and thin cotton pants. If she had been anyone else, he would've cursed her out for scaring him like this. But instead he forced himself to remain calm. It was a form of control he wasn't used to.

"Ma, we need to go home," he said.

She followed him, rubbing her arms as she walked.

"It's much colder here than I remember," she said.

Bruce hadn't mentioned any of this to his friends. It wasn't so much a decision he'd made, as something that happened by default. There never seemed to be a right time to bring it up. How do you go from boasting about some insane sex to commiserating about your sick mom? Bruce also feared that discussing it would give the situation a sense of permanence, like this was now the state of his life. He wasn't ready to think about it like that. Not yet. He wanted to maintain his old lifestyle as long as he could, but that was becoming increasingly challenging to do.

That night, he'd been planning to meet Michael and Sidney at the Mirror Ball. But when he arrived home from the gym around 10:00 pm, he knew something was wrong even before he opened the front door. He could hear the honking blare of the smoke alarm.

Bruce rushed in the house, and his nose was stung by black smoke coming from the kitchen. He dropped his gym bag at the front door and raced to the stove, where a huge pot of spaghetti sauce—always one of his mother's staples—was bubbling over. Burnt patches of sauce caked the stovetop.

Bruce turned off the stove, pushed open the window above the sink, and looked for his mother.

"Ma," he called as he went from room to room. She wasn't in the living room, but the TV was tuned to one of those home shopping networks she always watched. He had to remember to make sure that she didn't have access to any credit cards he didn't know about.

He looked in his bedroom, which was just off from the living room. She wasn't there, but he noticed that his bed had been made.

He then raced to the bedroom. He entered and saw his mother was asleep in her bed. She had always been able sleep through anything. At least that hadn't changed.

Chapter 10

The following Thursday, Ziggy walked from his dorm to a Cambodian restaurant on Wickenden where he was meeting Michael for their first date. The whole concept of a date was so odd to Ziggy. He wasn't completely sure why he was going on this date. The only thing he knew was that it was different, and he kinda liked doing things that were different.

Ziggy arrived at the restaurant and took great care to pull open the wooden door slowly. He didn't want to seem overzealous. Hell, he didn't even want to seem 'zealous.' As in all things, he wanted to play it cool.

There was a small wood paneled counter in the front of the restaurant and a bunch of round tables with floral tablecloths behind it. Ziggy looked around. Of the 10 diners in the restaurant, none were Michael.

He looked at his iPhone. It was already almost 7 minutes after 6:00 p.m. when they were supposed to meet up. "What if Michael stood him up?" Ziggy thought. In that instance, Ziggy knew why so many people hated dating. Dating was lame because you had to go out on a limb and expect another person to show up. You had to, like, care.

"May I help you?" asked a pretty Asian woman who'd just walked to the front of the counter.

Ziggy felt a little panicked. He put both hands in the pockets of his skinny gray jeans, slouched a bit and moved toward the counter. "Yeah, I just—" he was about to say "wanted to order some take-out," but a voice behind him said "Hey, man."

He turned and it was Michael, dressed in black jeans and a Wu-Tang hoodie. It took everything in Ziggy's power not to smile.

"What's up?" Ziggy said, giving Michael a friendly hug.

"Two," Michael told the hostess at the counter.

She led them to a table by the front window, handed them menus, and told them that their server would soon be with them.

"Sorry, I'm so late," Michael said, situating himself in his seat.

"No problem," Ziggy said, still recovering from the idea of being stood up.

"I mean, I probably would've been a few minutes late anyway because no one wants to be first to show up for a date." Michael laughed.

"Tell me about it, dick?" Ziggy kicked Michael under the table.

"No, the weirdest thing happened," Michael said, "I was looking for a place to park and I drove past where my friend Bruce–you know, the cop–where he lives."

"Yeah, I know the guy," Ziggy said.

(What he didn't tell Michael is that Bruce was always hitting on him, grabbing his ass at Mirror Ball and shit.

"What's with that guy," Ziggy once complained to his friend Andy, the shot boy.

"Ha! He does that to all the new twinks. He's a security guard or something at Johnson and Wales," Andy explained.

"I wish he'd knock it the fuck off," Ziggy said. "He's not my type at all."

"Too old?" Andy asked.

"Too cop.")

"So, anyway," Michael continued. "I thought I saw this old lady standing in the front yard of Bruce's house, and I was like, 'who the fuck is that?' I tried to stop, but there was this asshole in a huge RAM truck behind me beeping."

Ziggy nodded his head.

"It took me forever to go around the block again. I had to miss all kinds of parking spaces, but I was trying to figure out who this lady was."

"Did you figure it out," Ziggy asked. He looked up from the menu.

"No, she wasn't there when I drove back around," Michael said. "Maybe I got the houses mixed up."

Ziggy shrugged. They continued looking over the menu and decided on bubble teas and two tofu dishes since Michael was pescetarian and Ziggy had recently turned vegetarian.

"Yeah," Ziggy explained. "I heard it improves the taste of your spunk. I figure that vegetarian food is like mouthwash for your dick."

Michael laughed.

"You'll thank me later," Ziggy said. He noticed a pinkish hue appear on Michael's gingerbread colored cheeks.

Ziggy and Michael talked quick and easy as they waited for their food to arrive. They discovered that each of them hailed from Maryland. Ziggy explained that he was on partial scholarship at RISD.

Michael then shared his Providence origin story while they sipped their bubble teas: how he'd been a successful photo editor in New York, but gave up his career in order to be a full-time artist in Providence.

"How old are you, anyway," Ziggy asked. "You've lived like 2 lives."

"39," Michael said.

Ziggy did a spit take with his watermelon bubble tea. One bubble nearly popped Michael in the eye.

"Jesus!" Ziggy said.

"No," Michael said. "Jesus actually died around 33."

Ziggy still had his mouth open.

"I told you I was a lot older, " Michael continued.

"Yeah, but you're, like, a whole 20-year-old person older," said Ziggy, taking a pull from his straw.

"Does that turn you off?" asked Michael.

"No," said Ziggy. "I mean, you don't look that old or, like, act it. Not that I know a lot of 39-year-olds to compare you with. I mean, except for my mom. And you're not like her because she's, like, my mom."

"I didn't mean to mislead or anything," Michael said.

"It's not some big deal," Ziggy said. "It's just weird to think about."

The food arrived in steaming ornate bowls. They each took large spoonfuls of tofu and rice and made colorful piles on their plates. For a few minutes they ate in silence until Ziggy looked up from his food and said, "Can I ask you something?"

"I think that's pretty much the point of a date," Michael teased.

"Does it, um, turn you on that I'm 19?"

Michael wiped his mouth with his napkin. "Fuck, yeah!" he said.

They both laughed.

"Why aren't you into guys your age?" Ziggy asked.

Michael didn't speak for a moment. "It's more like guys my age aren't into me," he explained. "Or it's also like that."

"What do you mean?" Ziggy asked.

"I don't know. A lot of guys my age, and even younger, are, like, looking to shack up and settle down. They want to stop going out and, I dunno, sit on the couch and watch Netflix for the rest of their lives. But that's not me. I don't ever want to settle down. I don't even like that word, "settle." Who the fuck wants to "settle?"

"So why even bother dating and trying to have a boyfriend at all? Why not just hookup?"

"I dunno," Michael said. "It's cool to have someone regular sometimes. I'm not that into the hunt."

Ziggy nodded between forkfuls of tofu.

"It's also nice to have a designated parking spot for your dick," Michael joked.

Ziggy laughed.

"I don't know," Michael said. "It's complicated."

"That's why I mostly just hook up," Ziggy said. "It ain't complicated."

Michael shrugged.

The waiter came back to the table and cleared the plates, which were nearly scrubbed clean save for some stray traces of rice and yellow gravy. Soon afterward, the check came and Ziggy reached for it quickly.

"Split-sies?" Ziggy asked.

"I got it," Michael said, slipping his credit card into the bill holder.

"If you're paying, I suppose I have to put out," Ziggy said. He noticed Michael's face flushing again.

They left the restaurant and walked to Michael's car, a banana-yellow Honda Fit.

"Give you a ride back to your dorm?" Michael asked.

"Or your place?" Ziggy often found that eating made him horny.

"Told you I'm not really the hook-up type."

"Who said anything about hooking up?" Ziggy said as he started to feel his dick pushing against his boxers. "I wanna see some of your work."

"Really?" Michael asked. His face brightened.

"Yeah," Ziggy said, adjusting himself.

They got into the car. Michael started it up and pushed the power button on the radio. The oldies hip-hop station was playing The Notorious B.I.G.'s "Warning".

"Oh, this is my *shit*," Ziggy yelled, turning up the volume. "When I was little, I stole this CD from my babysitter." Ziggy started rhyming with the song: "Remember them niggas from the hill up in Brownsville that you rolled dice with, smoked blunts and got nice with?"

Ziggy pointed at Michael, who came in. "Yeah, my nigga Fame up in Prospect. Nah, them my niggas. Nah, love wouldn't disrespect…"

Ziggy continued: "I didn't say them. They schooled me to some niggas that you knew from back when, when you was clockin' minor figures. Now they heard you're blowing up like nitro and they wanna stick the knife through your windpipe slow…"

They went on laughing and trading verses until the song was over.

"This is literally the hardest thing my butt has ever been on, and that's saying something," Ziggy said once they arrived at Michael's apartment. They were seated on his living room sofa.

"Fuck off," Michael said, punching Ziggy in the arm. "It was just some cheap thing that I got from Ikea. I didn't have a lot of money for furniture when I moved in."

"So, let's see your pictures then," Ziggy said.

"Really?"

"Yeah."

"Are you sure? I mean, you don't have to do it because you think it's polite or something."

"No, I really want to see them. Why are you being a weirdo?"

"I dunno," Michael said. "Most guys who come over… I mean, not that *that* many guys come over… but most don't ever ask to see my work. They don't really give a shit."

"So what?" Ziggy said.

"I dunno. I just think it's weird when people act like they wanna get to know me, but they don't ask about what I do, which is kinda my passion."

"Yeah, I get that," Ziggy said.

"You know Robert Mapplethorpe?" Michael asked.

"Sure," Ziggy said. "Leather dudes. Flowers. That one picture with the whip up his ass…"

"Yeah, well, he was best friends with this singer, Patti Smith—"

"My mom likes her." Ziggy said.

"Well, when people asked Patti how they could get close to Robert, she'd just say, 'love his work.'"

Ziggy nodded.

"I mean, it's not that my work is all that matters," Michael said. "But it's what matters to the core, you know?"

Ziggy did know. He could really relate to Michael, and it made him feel...well, he wasn't exactly sure how to describe the feeling. It was like a combination of drinking a cup of hot chocolate and watching one of those YouTube videos where soldiers are reunited with their dogs.

Ziggy swallowed. "Alright already. Are you gonna show me your pictures or what? I feel like I'm at one of those movies where there are 45 minutes of previews."

Michael got up from the couch and grabbed his black leather portfolio from a bookshelf. He handed it to Ziggy, who put it on his lap. Ziggy started to open the portfolio, but stopped suddenly.

"What if I think your stuff sucks?" Ziggy asked.

"If you wanna make it out of here alive, you better keep it to yourself," Michael said with a forced smile.

Ziggy laughed. "You don't want feedback?"

"Not if it's negative." Michael said.

"You wouldn't have made it very far in art school," Ziggy said.

"It's like what the author Truman Capote used to say, 'Once I've finished a book, all I want is praise.'"

"O.K.," said Ziggy. "I'll just stick to what I like and what I really like."

"Deal," Michael said.

Ziggy opened the book. The first image was a close-up of an strikingly beautiful young man's face; his mouth was open seductively; a stream of cigarette smoke spiraled from his lips. The next image was of the same tough yet dreamy guy with a swirl of city lights forming a halo around his head. Page after page, the same face appeared.

"Who's this dude?" Ziggy asked Michael, who was on the other side of the room flipping through an Avedon monograph.

"Who?" Michael asked.

"Duh, him," Ziggy said, pointing to a picture. "He's on, like, every other page."

"That's Chase," Michael said without really needing to look.

"You obviously had a huge thing for him."

Michael shrugged.

"Were you guys, like, together?" Ziggy asked.

"Not really," Michael said, looking back at Ziggy. "Sometimes. I mean, we were close. But he was straight. *Is* straight. He had a girlfriend."

"But you loved him, right?"

Michael was silent.

"Man," said Ziggy, "you don't even have to say anything. I can tell by the way you're acting."

Michael shrugged again.

"Where is he now?" Ziggy asked.

"Not sure."

"Maybe he'll come back," Ziggy said.

"Maybe it's time for me to move on." Michael said.

Ziggy went back to flipping through the portfolio.

"How old is he in these pictures?"

"I don't know," Michael said. "19, maybe?"

"Have a type much?" Ziggy joked.

Michael flipped him the finger.

"So, when do I get to see your work?" Michael asked.

Ziggy pulled his iPhone out of his pocket, punched up a photo gallery, and handed it to Michael.

"This is some shit I've been working on," Ziggy said. "And you can actually tell me what you really think about it. *I'm not a pussy…or some non-sexist equivalent.*"

Michael gave him a puzzled look.

"One of my electives is Intro to Women's Studies," Ziggy explained.

Michael swiped through the photos and used his fingers to enlarge some of them.

"These are cool," Michael said. "It looks like barren trees or bushes. Are they burning?"

"Yeah," Ziggy said, "they're my pubes, close up, with some Instagram filters. I think my bush looks best in Amaro."

"You lit your pubes on fire?"

"Anything for art," Ziggy said, pulling down the front of his low-hanging jeans. "It's still pretty barren down there."

"You nut job," Michael said. He handed the phone back to Ziggy.

"It was for a school assignment: The Personal Landscape." Ziggy closed Michael's portfolio and placed it on a small coffee table. Talking about pubes was making Ziggy horny again.

"You know, this is the part where we should start making out and having wild, artsy sex," he said.

"I'm not ready yet, dude," Michael said. He walked to the other side of the room.

"Why?" asked Ziggy

"I dunno," Michael said. "I just don't want to be your one-time, old-guy fling. I mean, I wish I could be like every other homo and just fuck on demand, but I can't. I've never been able to. Sex brings up all kinds of feels for me."

Ziggy had a hard time processing what he was hearing. It wasn't that he didn't believe Michael; he had just never heard anyone say something like this before. He also couldn't relate.

For Ziggy, sex had always been about sensation. From the first time his 13-year-old dick issued a watery dribble of cum, he'd been obsessed with finding all the things he could do to his body to make it feel good. He experimented with multiple ways to jerk off: the left handed method, the bed grind, the lotion-filled sock, and so on.

Then he moved to exploring his ass. At the time, he didn't know if he was a top or bottom, but he thought it was best to ne prepared for any possibility. That was his one takeaway from a week-long stint in the Boy Scouts.

Ziggy tried to stick a carrot up his ass, but found it too pointy. Then he shoved a rather large, dry cucumber up his butt, and it hurt so much that he couldn't shit for a week. It was an early lesson in the importance of lube.

A short time later, his mom went on a health kick and stopped buying vegetables that had been drenched in pesticides or cultivated for enlargement. Ziggy quickly discovered that when it came to insertable produce, his butthole preferred organic.

Ziggy's early sexual experiences mostly involved friends, a couple of the butch-er members of his high school's Drama Club, and a large percentage of both the Swim and

Gymnastics teams. He never had trouble finding someone to fool around with.

But as he got older, he began to realize that, for all the fantastic, tingly, squirty, stretchy things he was experiencing, there were other things that he wasn't feeling, things he'd never experienced. He'd think about this sometimes when he saw couples cuddling on that patch of grass on Benefit St. between Waterman and Angell. He'd also think about it when one of his friends would cry over a breakup. He'd wonder how someone else—a non-family someone—could affect you so deeply. Ziggy realized that he had never let someone touch him beyond the surface layer of the skin, reaching something deeper, something unexplored and as fragile as a newborn. Ziggy knew that if he ever let this happen, it would be like losing his virginity again— his *butt* virginity. If this was going to happen, he wanted it to be with someone experienced, someone gentle, someone safe.

Ziggy said, "I've never said this before in my fucking life, but I'll wait until you're ready."

Part Four

Chapter 11

On an unseasonably warm Saturday night in November, Dante arrived at Sidney's apartment panting and wiping sweat from his forehead. It reminded Sidney of how he looked after sex.

"Sorry I'm late," Dante said, as Sidney pulled him into a tight hug. "It's mad-crowded out there."

Sidney kissed Dante long, soft, and slow. Then he gave him a hard smack on the ass as they walked into the guest bedroom.

"Yeah, it's Waterfire tonight," Sidney said, leading Dante into the spare bedroom. "When I first moved here, I went all the time. I loved the primal strangeness of the whole thing, all those people mesmerized by the river on fire. But now I barely glance out the window when it's happening. I can't even tell you the last time I've been."

"I've never been," said Dante. He put his messenger bag on the floor.

Sidney stopped turning down the sheets.

"Never?" Sidney said, "I thought you grew up in Providence."

"Yeah," said Dante, "But not over this way."

Sidney nodded.

"When shit's on fire in my hood, it ain't nothing to celebrate."

Sidney laughed.

"We should go," Sidney said.

Dante stopped unzipping his jeans. "Now?" he asked.

"Yeah," Sidney said. "You should experience it at least once in your life."

"And what about…" Dante pointed to his crotch.

"Later," Sidney said.

Sidney and Dante walked out of Sidney's building and down the stone steps into Providence River Park. All around were people staring at piles of wood burning in metal wire baskets in the middle of the river. They continued walking, as the path changed from cobblestones to brick and they made their way past several RISD buildings. The crowd was a mix of hand-holding couples, young and old; impassive college kids paying more attention to their phones than the fire; parents rolling children in elephantine strollers; and dewy faced teens intoxicated by being on their own in the night.

As a tide of faces rushed by, Sidney briefly feared that he would run into someone he knew. How would he explain Dante? But then Sidney realized that no explanation would be necessary. People would see an older gay gentleman with someone much younger and do the math; nothing Sidney could do or say would stop two and two from equaling four.

"It smells like Christmas," Dante said.

"What?" Sidney asked, snapping back to the moment.

"The smell in the air," Dante said. He took a deep whiff of burning pine. "It's like Christmas."

Sidney laughed. "I guess it is."

"Yeah," Dante said. "When I was a kid, we used to have a house, and we'd always have a fresh tree at Christmas."

"What happened?" Sidney asked.

"Typical hood shit," Dante said. "Dad peaced out. Mom couldn't keep up with the bills. Next thing you know, no more house."

"Sorry to hear that."

Dante shrugged.

"What does your mom do now?"

"She's on disability. I try to help her out whenever I can."

"Is that why you started…"

"Tricking? Yeah. I mean, I needed the money."

"And you obviously enjoyed it," Sidney said.

"Well, the weird thing is that tricking actually made me cool with being with guys. I always felt that maybe I wanted to experiment. But I didn't really know how to go about it, you know. So tricking, in a way, helped me get to know myself better."

Sidney nodded.

"But, more and more," Dante continued. "I'm starting to think it's time for something else."

Sidney felt a tightening in his gut.

They arrived back at Sidney's apartment, fucked madly, and afterward stayed in bed holding each other longer than they ever had before. At one point, Dante got up to piss, and when he came back to bed, he didn't get in front of Sidney as usual, but instead got behind him and curled his arm across Sidney's thick, round chest. Sidney felt a flash of indignation at first, but then he slowly gave in to a feeling that was rare for him: surrender.

The next morning, Sidney leaned against the kitchen counter dazedly watching coffee brew in his Moccamaster. The pot filled and Sidney poured the coffee into a large, white ceramic mug, added two scoops of sugar, and a healthy dose of half and half. He watched as the light brown mixture swirled around in his cup and then peacefully settled as if it had never been touched.

Dante walked in. "What's up?" he said.

"Oh nothing," said Sidney, "I just need to get myself going for work."

"It's Sunday," said Dante.

"Yeah, but my assistant just called... well, she called earlier... she emailed me last night... texted and said that she couldn't open today and–"

"Yo, if you want me to go, just tell me to go. All this made-up shit is corny."

Sidney stood up and placed his hands on Dante's bare shoulders. "I don't want you to go, but I need you to go."

"Why?" Dante said, breaking away from Sidney's grip. "We had a great time last night. That's why I want you to stop fucking paying me. I want to be with you, just you. You're the first guy I've said that to."

"That's the thing," said Sidney calmly as he sipped from his cup. "I'm not trying to be somebody's first boyfriend. The shit never works out, and I'm not gonna to put myself through all that."

"But I'm not like everybody else."

Sidney moved toward Dante and kissed him lightly on the lips. "I know you believe that, baby. But every guy who's ever done me wrong has said the same damn thing."

"I don't get it," Dante said. "What are you so afraid of?"

"Afraid?" Sidney laughed heartily. "I'm afraid of what every other motherfucker is afraid of. I'm afraid of looking like a goddamned fool."

"As long as you know what you want," Dante said, turning back toward the guest bedroom.

"I know what I can live with."

Chapter 12

It was 12:45 am and Traci was laying in her bed unable to sleep. None of her usual cures for insomnia were working—not the DVR marathon of *Scandal*, the attempt to make it through an entire issue of *The New Yorker*, or the two cocktails she made of vodka and Diet Cranberry Snapple. If anything, it seemed like her aggressive attempts to go to sleep were keeping her up.

She wondered if Ziggy was still up. Actually, she *knew* he was still up. Ziggy had exhibited vampire-like sleep tendencies since birth. But she wondered if he'd be in a mood to hear from his mother. Feeling emboldened, probably from the booze, she grabbed her phone from the nightstand and dialed.

"Hey," Ziggy answered on first ring. He sounded so welcoming that she wondered for a moment if he thought the call was from someone else.

"Uh, hi," she said, sitting up in bed and muting the TV.

"You're up late." Ziggy said.

"Couldn't sleep. Figured you'd be up. Thought I'd see how things were going." She twisted one of her forefingers as if twirling an old telephone cord.

"I'm working on a project that's due Monday. It's kind of a collage of all the cartoon guys that I've wanted to hook up with over the years: Otto from *Rocket Power*, Trent from *Daria*, Gerald, the guy with the ill high-top-fade from *Hey Arnold!*, Connor from *Young Justice*, and a whole bunch of other animated studs that I thought were hot when I was growing up."

Traci was struck by the phrase "when I was growing up." She realized, perhaps for the first time, that Ziggy now thought of himself as an adult, grown. She remembered thinking the same thing at his age. It was funny how, as the years go by, the confident feeling of being done with—fully cooked—slowly gives way to the realization that you're never more than a work in progress.

"What else is going on?" Traci asked.

"Nothing. You know, stuff."

"Are you still seeing that guy? What was his name? Diego?" She leaned forward on the bed.

"I wasn't *seeing* him, mom. We just hooked up."

"All you ever talk about is hooking up," she said. "Don't people date anymore?"

"Who says I'm not dating?"

Traci sat up again. "Are you?"

"Maybe. I don't know."

"What's not to know?" she asked.

Ziggy laughed. "There's this guy I met. We're sorta seeing where things might go. We're taking it slow."

"*You're* taking something slow?" She had to laugh.

"I know, right. Shocker," Ziggy said. "But he wanted to. And, I don't know, it's something I'm trying out."

"Does he have a name?"

"Of course, mother," Ziggy said. "Most people find that a name is a socially useful thing to have."

"Well, what is his name, smartass?"

"Eh, I don't really want to talk about it too much. Not yet."

"You don't want to jinx it?" she asked, finding herself torn between mom-advisory-mode and gushy boy-talk mode.

"No," Ziggy said. "I don't want you asking about him until the end of time if it doesn't work out."

Traci didn't respond. The key to getting Ziggy to divulge information was to seem as disinterested as possible. Traci glanced at the DVR clock and decided not to speak again until the timer changed from 12:52 to 12:53.

"O.K.," Ziggy continued. "I'll tell you one thing, just because it's a little different for me."

Traci, still watching the clock, forced herself to remain quiet.

"He's kinda older. Well, a lot kinda."

"Older?" Traci couldn't stop herself.

"Not like gross Hugh Hefner older. More like Ashton and Demi, before they got divorced."

"Jesus!" Her hand stopped twirling the imaginary cord and moved to clutching imaginary pearls.

"See, that's why I don't tell you stuff. You always react like that."

"Like what?" Traci asked. She got up from the bed and pressed her hand against the dresser.

"Like all hysterical."

"I'm just surprised," she said, starting to pace.

"It's not some creepy "Daddy" situation," Ziggy said. "It's like he's older, but doesn't really seem older, if you know what I mean?"

She didn't, but she didn't want to come off as judgmental.

"Well, as long as you…" She wasn't sure what else to say.

"It works for me, for now," Ziggy said.

She wanted to wrap the conversation up before she said the wrong thing, something questioning or disapproving which would make Ziggy double down in whatever this May-December thing was. Her head was frothing over with wrong things to say.

"Well, I'll let you get back to your project," she said.

"O.K., "Ziggy said. "I love you and stuff."

Her heart broke a little. She sat back on the bed. "I love you and stuff too."

Chapter 13

While Ziggy talked to his mother, Michael was headed

to the Mirror Ball after receiving the following text from Bruce:

"@ MB. Need 2 tell u some shit. Drop by if u can." Michael had

planned to stay in that night since Ziggy was working on a

project. But Bruce's text sounded serious. Rarely did the word

"need" come up in one of Bruce's communiqués.

Michael arrived on the second floor balcony and spotted

Bruce with his shirt off, looking down at the dance floor. A

bottle of Poland Spring stuck out of his back pocket. This meant

he'd probably been drinking a lot.

Michael came up from behind him and playfully smacked his butt.

Bruce turned toward him. "Oh, hey," he said, blankly.

"What's up?"

"Same shit." Bruce said. He grabbed his t-shirt from the waistband of his jeans. "Let's go upstairs."

On the top floor, a musician played Elton John's "I Guess That's Why They Call It The Blues" on the piano. Michael and Bruce went to the bar and ordered a Absolut Vanilla Vodka with Diet Coke and a Bud Light respectively. Then they moved to a couple of leather chairs by a large bay window.

Bruce stared into the dark outside for a while and then said, "You know how people always say that they don't want to die alone, that they're scared of it?"

"Uh, yeah," Michael said. Bruce's tone made him uneasy.

"Well, dying alone—like the whole idea of it—doesn't really bother me. I figure most of us are gonna die alone anyways, like if you figure the odds. Even in a married couple, somebody's gotta die first, right? Then the other person's gonna be alone. I mean, I suppose there could be some kind of freak accident and they go at the same time. But you get my point…"

"Yeah," said Michael. "I mean, I guess."

"My point is that dying alone isn't the thing that scares me. I don't ever think about it, not at all."

Michael nodded.

"But sometimes," Bruce continued, "sometimes I find myself thinking that I don't want to be alone *before* I die, you know, like while I'm still living."

"But you always have guys around," Michael said, feeling a bit unnerved by Bruce's uncharacteristic mood.

"Yeah, but that's different," Bruce said. "Now don't get me wrong. I love fucking. I love meeting a hot new guy, some twink, and fucking his brains out. I love that, really love that. But…" Bruce stopped.

A few moments of silence passed.

"What?" Michael said. "You think you want a boyfriend or something?"

Bruce didn't answer right away. He leaned forward and looked at Michael. Bruce opened his mouth as if to say something, but then he closed it. He put his hands on his knees and slumped down until his neck touched the top of the chair.

"I don't know what I fucking want," Bruce said.

Michael took another sip from his drink. He wasn't used to Bruce being so heavy.

"I guess I understand where you're coming from," Michael said, "like feeling that you want something more."

Bruce looked up.

"There's this guy I'm seeing—" Michael continued.

Bruce shot up in his chair. "You're seeing someone?"

"Sorta. I mean, I'm not exactly sure how to describe—."

"When did this happen?" Bruce asked, his voice slowly rising.

"What?"

"Like fucking all of it," Bruce said, loudly.

"I don't know. I guess it's been the better part of a month now."

"Were you ever gonna fucking tell me?" Bruce asked.

"I'm telling you now."

"I know you're telling me now, asshole." Bruce grabbed his beer and took a long pull.

"What's your problem?" Michael asked.

"My problem is all this secretive shit," Bruce said. He started tapping his right foot.

"It's not like I was trying to keep it some big secret. You haven't been around as much lately and—"

"And that's my fucking fault?" Bruce said. His voice rose again. Other people in the bar looked their way.

"I'm not saying it's your fault. I just haven't seen you as much. We haven't really talked."

"This is such bullshit." Bruce slammed his beer against the table again.

"I don't see why you're so upset."

"Of course, you don't. Your head's so far up your own fucking ass—"

"I'm sorry I didn't tell you, O.K.? Fucking jeez."

Bruce said nothing.

They stayed silent while they finished their drinks. Michael looked over at Bruce, whose face seemed to have softened. Perhaps the alcohol had kicked in and had a calming effect.

"Friends?" Michael said, attempting to lighten the mood.

Bruce's face tightened again.

"There are no fucking friends," Bruce spat. "There are just some people that you think you know better than others, but it always turns out that you don't know shit."

"That's pretty harsh."

"It is what it is."

"Well, I'm sorry you feel this way." Michael said.

"I'm sorry fucking life's this way." Bruce stood to leave.

"Wait. You said you wanted to tell me something?" Michael asked.

"Yeah," Bruce said. "Fuck off."

Chapter 14

The next afternoon, Michael arrived at Sidney's waterfront gallery to pick up a check. He walked through the glass doors and saw Sidney with an extremely thin man in a tailored suit. They were standing in front of a small, framed photo. Sidney spotted Michael and waved him over.

"Wesley," Sidney said to the man next to him, "I want to introduce you to someone."

Sidney placed his hand on Michael's shoulder. "This is Michael Allen. He's a photographer. I've shown you his work in the past."

The two shook hands.

"Of course," said the Wesley to Michael. "You did that great, b&w picture of the skinny little guy with the hairy, little asshole."

Michael nodded. He knew he was talking about a picture of Chase. "I remember that one."

"One?" Sidney quipped. "Michael has done so many asshole photos that I could cover my walls top to, well, bottom."

Michael glared at Sidney.

"I wanted to buy it," said Wesley, "but I wasn't sure where I'd put it in the house. My partner entertains a lot, Democratic Party stuff. I felt it might be too much ass for mixed company."

"I understand," Michael said. He'd heard this kind of thing from collectors before.

"I'm definitely interested in seeing more from you, though," Wesley said. "Are you working on something now?"

"Oh, you know," said Michael, "more guys, more ass, a low-hanging ball or two."

"Lovely," Wesley chimed. "You know, there's always been something I wanted to ask photographers like you, those who do nudes and such with the pretty young men. I've always wondered if relationships develop or if you ever, um…"

"Have sex?" Sidney inserted.

"Yes," Wesley said. "Do you ever have sex with your subjects?"

Michael blushed. "Sometimes it just happens."

"And the boy with the hairy little asshole?" queried Wesley.

"That was different," Michael said. "It wasn't about sex so much. It was—"

"Sounds like you were in love," said Wesley.

"He definitely was," Sidney said.

Michael shifted on his feet. "It's hard to explain. I met him when I first moved here, when I was just trying to establish myself as a photographer. He trusted me, believed in me. There's a special feeling you have for someone who helps you become what you want to be."

"Do you still see him?" Wesley asked.

"No. I don't really know where he is right now. I wish I did, but—"

"Oh," Wesley exclaimed, "but you have all of your beautiful photographs to remember him by." Wesley bounced up and down on the heels of his Prada loafers. "That's so romantic. I just have to buy the hairy little asshole picture right now. Is it still available?"

"Certainly," Sidney said.

Wesley continued, "I'll just have to find a creative place to hang it. The husband will be peeved, of course. But screw him, I need some romance in my life."

"Well, thank you," Michael said, surprised.

"You're quite welcome, my boy," Wesley said, as he grasped Michael's forearms and looked in his eyes. "And I hope…I hope you find the boy—your boy—again. I can see that what you feel for him is real, and, take it from an old queen, those kind of feelings are rare in a lifetime. Don't let them go without a fight."

Michael smiled and began to back away, but Wesley gripped his forearms more firmly. He was surprisingly strong for a frail-looking man.

"See, the thing people get wrong about aging is that they think staying young is all about moisturizers, Botox, and all those goddamn Acai berries that are in everything these days. But the real key to staying young, to feeling young, is to never lose faith in possibilities, to never give up on the idea that fantastic things await. *That* is the great fight."

"See," Wesley continued, "that's what your hairy asshole...or rather, the boy's hairy asshole...the *photo* of the hairy asshole, that's what it means to me. It speaks to me about love and hope, which is to say life."

"Thanks," Michael said, as Wesley let go of his arms. "I mean, thanks again."

"Michael," Sidney said, "why don't you wait for me in my office while I finish up with Wesley?"

"O.K.," Michael said.

Michael told Wesley goodbye and headed into Sidney's office. He sat on the sleek, white couch, picked up a copy of *Artforum* from the coffee table and then put it right back down.

All he could think about now was Chase. The conversation with Wesley was jarring, but not necessarily painful. It made him realize how much time and passed since he'd thought about Chase in any sustained way. Not long ago, the idea of getting through a day without thinking about Chase seemed the biggest of impossibilities, like ice dancing on the sun. But somehow it had happened. He didn't think about Chase all the time anymore, not even everyday. Was the change simply due simply to the intangible way that time can erode even the sharpest emotional edges? Or was the change due to something more tangible—Ziggy?

A few minutes later, Sidney walked in the office, sat behind his glass desk and sighed. "Sorry for all that."

"All what?" Michael asked.

"All of Wesley. He's always going on and on about something—love, the meaning of life, his distrust of the medicinal properties of Acai berries. He's a great customer, but he can be trying at times. Most times."

"At least he bought something."

"True," said Sidney. "You're well on your way to cornering the hirsute anus market."

"I can't believe he found that picture so romantic," Michael said, leaning back on the couch, "or at least the idea of it."

"What do you mean?"

"It's just interesting how people can view things in your life differently than you do. Like the situation with Chase, it doesn't feel romantic to me. At least not anymore. It just feels…It just feels like something gone. And the surprising thing is that it doesn't hurt as much anymore. It's like I've gotten used to it."

"It's 'cause you have a new boy to occupy your mind."

Michael blushed.

"So, little Michael is happy at last? Merriam-Webster will have to remove your photo from their entry on 'melancholia.'"

"Whatever," said Michael, laughing. "Not everything is great. There was this shit with Bruce last night."

"What happened?"

"Fuck if I know. I was telling him about Ziggy and he went all kinds of ape shit."

"You know he's in love with you, right?" Sidney said, matter-of-factly.

"Shut the fuck up. He so is not."

"I'm not saying that Bruce knows what he's feeling. I'm just saying that the feelings are there. Otherwise, why would he give a fuck?"

"But what about all the other guys he's fucking?"

"This isn't about fucking," Sidney said. "You're the one he trusts, the one he lets in. That means more than all the young guys who are stuck to his shaft like twink-sicles?"

"How can I make it right?" Michael asked.

"There's really nothing to do except wait until he gets his shit together. It could be a long wait."

Sidney shuffled some papers on his desk, looking for Michael's check.

"And what's up with you?," Michael asked. "Have you seen that guy again?"

"I told you that I wasn't seeing him anymore," Sidney said.

"Have you seen any other guys?" Michael said, punctuating 'guys' with air quotes.

"No need for hand gestures," Sidney said. "There are a couple of new guys on RentMe that I've tried out. Had to pay extra for them to Uber from Springfield, but whatever."

"Well, that's what you like, right? Variety. Easy go, easy, um, cum."

Sidney grabbed a stress ball from his desk and aimed it at Michael's head.

"Ouch," Michael said as the ball hit him right above his right eye. "All I meant was, 'you're happy, right?'"

Sidney raised his arms. "Happy? Unhappy? Who the fuck knows? Whatever I'm feeling is familiar. I know what it is. So, in that sense, it's good."

"But is it really enough?"

"What, are you about to dispense life advice? Let me grab a pad."

"Just hear me out. The thing about spending time with Ziggy is that I'm starting to see a lot of shit differently. It's like, we can go through life thinking that we're the happiest we can ever be, or that we've already been the happiest we ever will be, but then something unexpected can happen that can make you feel happier or, like, give you the idea that you could one day *be* happier. It's like you think your life is stuck at one volume and then someone turns it up."

"Sounds like a fucking headache."

"Seriously, don't you want something like that? Don't you want, like, more."

"Depends on how much it costs."

Chapter 15

A couple of nights after his meeting with Sidney, Michael was sitting in his apartment feeling hornier than he'd felt in a while. It was a very specific type of horny, not the kind that jerking off would satiate. Michael wanted to touch and be touched; to taste; to have those moments of anticipation where you don't know where someone's finger, tongue, or dick was going to go next. Michael wanted sex, and he decided that he wanted it with Ziggy.

Over the weeks since they'd been dating, Michael had come to more clarity about why he'd wanted to take things slow with Ziggy. It wasn't just that he wasn't that into hook-ups. That was true to a point. But the number of exceptions he'd made to that principle exceeded anything he could count with his fingers and toes. What he realized was that he had wanted to wait because of how much he liked Ziggy. He knew that if Ziggy had quickly broken things off with him after a few fuck-filled nights, he'd be back in that dark place where he'd resided for so long after losing Chase. He wasn't ready to return there.

But tonight, Michael felt almost as if his extreme horniness was a sign that he was ready to take the risk with Ziggy, a sign that he would be resilient enough to survive if the risk didn't yield longterm rewards. Something in him felt healed and strengthened.

"I'm ready," Michael texted Ziggy.

Less than a minute later, Ziggy texted back: "Be there by 8." Next to the words were three eggplant emojis.

Michael replied, "k."

Michael felt giddy for a moment, but then a mild panic set in. It was 6 pm. He had two hours to eat dinner, straighten up the apartment, change the linens on the bed, and make sure that condoms and lube were conveniently but not too conspicuously stashed in the top drawer of the nightstand.

In addition to everything else, Michael wanted to squeeze in some push-ups and crunches. He felt he had to be ever vigilant to stave off the middle-aged body's tendency toward puffiness or deflation.

Lastly, he needed to groom, a process that took longer with each passing year. Potentially embarrassing things increasingly seemed to be sprouting out of him, like the hair that now grew around the tops of his ears and on the inner lobe.

Then, when the presence of hair wasn't causing problems, it was the color of the hair or rather the lack of color. A few weeks ago, Michael looked in the mirror and thought he had something stuck in his nose. He blew his nose and was surprised when the thing was still there. He blew another time. Still there. He then made a sort of nose probe out of the tissue and stuck it all the way up his nostril, in and out, in and out. It was as if he were nose-fucking himself. He pulled the tissue out, tossed it in the trash and looked at his nostrils in the mirror again. The stringy white thing remained. Michael started to think that this particular nose-invader was made from some sort of Kleenex-resistant mutant mucous. But then he looked closer and realized that the shiny white thing wasn't a mucous at all, but rather a long gray hair that had taken up residence in his nose. A wave of grief and disgust came over him. Who even knew that you could get gray nose hairs?

He reached in the medicine cabinet for his tweezers, stuck them in his nose and plucked out a stiff, silvery strand of hair. He starred it down for a moment, almost as if he were in a standoff. He couldn't believe that this hair made him so furious. He was as embarrassed by his emotional response as he was by the hair itself. He decided at that moment that his approach to the unexpected curses of aging would be thoughtful strategy rather than spontaneous anger.

That was the reason why Michael was standing naked in front of his bathroom sink, mixing chemicals in a way that he hadn't since the days of his required college Chemistry. He was preparing a batch of hair dye for his pubes.

Michael had acquired gray pubes here and there in his early 30s. But it was nothing that a quick plucking couldn't handle. But in the past few months, an entire thatch of gray had sprouted up in his bush, and the hairs were concentrated in such a way that no degree of tweezing or trimming was going to diminish them. He could've completely shaved his pubes. But that look never worked for anyone over 25 or not in porn. The best option was to dye them. Unfortunately "Just For Men" didn't make a product "Just For Pubes," so Michael had to make do with the brush-in color gel for mustaches, beards, and sideburns.

Having never used the product before, Michael was surprised at all the components that came in the box: the multiple tubes, a comb, and something that looked like a doll-sized paint brush. He mixed the "Color Bare" tube with the "Color Developer" tube in a small plastic tray that came in the box. He then used the brush applicator to liberally baste his bush. He wanted to make sure to get an even look. Any kind of discoloration in the pubic region was a sure mood killer.

Michael finished applying the mixture and checked himself out in the mirror. His newly gelled pubes gave him a moment of satisfaction. He had taken the first step toward ridding his crotch of the gray menace. But as he inspected himself a little more closely, his feeling of accomplishment was replaced by panic. In the process of putting the gel on his pubes, he'd gotten a considerable amount on his dick. His penis was now dotted with a series of dark misshapen brown patches.

Panic-stricken, Michael whipped off his gloves and jumped in the shower. He grabbed a bar of Irish Spring and frantically rubbed at his crotch. He hadn't applied this much friction to his groin since he was first learning to masturbate. He rubbed and rubbed and rubbed until the splotches on his dick started coming off. A rush of light brown water pooled at his feet. By the time he finished showering, his peen was back to normal and his pubes were the shiny dark brown of his 20s. Mission accomplished.

Just before Ziggy was to arrive, Michael took one last look at his naked self the mirror. He spritzed the air in front of him with Marc Jacob's Bang and stepped into the peppery spray. As he moved forward, the light hit his face in such a way that he noticed something shiny above his left eye. He moved closer to the mirror, and sure enough, he had one shimmering gray hair in the middle of his left eyebrow. He decided to leave it the fuck alone.

"So, this is kinda awkward, huh?" Michael said. Ziggy had just arrived at the apartment and was reclining on Michael's sofa with his feet on the coffee table. Michael sat on a nearby chair, leaning forward, bouncing his foot up and down.

"What's awkward about it?" Ziggy asked.

"I don't know. It just feels weird."

"Dude, I thought you said you were ready. Why are you freaking out again?"

"I dunno. The whole not-wanting-to-get-hurt thing."

"Dude, you are honestly too much," Ziggy said, laughing.

"I'm just me." Michael said.

"O.K., look, I'll show you how serious I am," Ziggy said, pulling out his phone. His fingers swept across the screen for several seconds.

"Now check your Facebook," Ziggy said.

Michael pulled out his iPhone and opened Facebook. Under "Notifications," it said "Ziggy Hunter has stated that you are in a relationship." Then it had buttons for "confirm" or "don't allow." Michael looked over at Ziggy, grinned, and pressed, "confirm."

"So now we're Facebook official," Ziggy said. "If things get any more serious, an ordained lesbian will have to be involved."

"Alright," said Michael. "I get the point."

"So, can we fuck already?" Ziggy said. "Seriously? This is the longest I've gone without sex since I don't fucking know when. Now I know how my mom feels when she's on Weight Watchers."

"Uh, we sorta have one more thing we need to talk about," Michael said.

"I'm negative," Ziggy said, "but I always use condoms anyway."

"I'm negative too, but that's not it. What I meant was, like, who's gonna do who?"

Ziggy laughed. "Are you gonna tell me you're a total top or something? I hear that was big in the '90s."

"See, here's the thing," Michael said. "It's not like I mind getting fucked if I'm in a relationship. Or, let me clarify, if I'm in a relationship that's more than a few minutes old. But my preference, like, in this particular case—"

"O.K., old man, you can fuck me. Now, let's get on with it, *please!*"

Ziggy stood up, took off his t-shirt, and threw it in Michael's face. He pulled his jeans down to his ankles and predictably wasn't wearing underwear. His dick was so erect that it looked like it was pointing to something in the left hand corner of the room. He kicked off his pants, and as they slid across the floor, his phone slipped out of his pocket and began buzzing wildly.

#

A few minutes earlier, Traci had just sat down in front of her Macbook to do her monthly bills. It was never fun to watch her money dribble away, so instead of going straight to Quicken, Traci checked her Facebook News Feed. She had some friends and work acquaintances who took offense if she didn't immediately "like" their family photos and amateur food porn.

At the top of the page, she saw a photo of her son. Seeing Ziggy's thumbnail made her smile, even though it was a photo of him with a fake bloody nose—or at least she hoped it was fake. She looked at his most recent update and read "Ziggy Hunter is now in a relationship with Michael Allen."

Traci's throat tightened and her hand shook as she clicked on Michael's name. She had to be sure it was her old college friend and not some person on the internet with the same name, a Googleganger. Michael's profile pic came up, and she recognized him instantly. Traci grabbed her phone and texted as fast as her trembling fingers could move: "CALL ME NOW. MICHAEL IS YOUR DAD."

Part Five

Chapter 16

Two days after his encounter with Ziggy, Michael sat

among the brunch crowd at Brickway on Wickenden, a cozy cafe

with great omelettes and colorful, swirling murals. Michael was

waiting for an old friend from college. He didn't know quite

what to expect from this most unusual reunion. After Ziggy

raced from his apartment the other evening with no explanation,

Michael received a Facebook message from a woman he'd been

close with when he went to the University of Maryland at

College Park. It read: "Hi Michael. It's Traci from college. I

need to speak with you as soon as possible. It's about Ziggy.

He's my son. I'll be in Providence tomorrow and would like to meet with you the following morning if possible. Please let me know."

Michael read those words and felt like someone hit him in the nuts with a mallot. "What the fuck?" he thought. Ziggy was Traci's kid? He knew she had a kid. He vaguely remembered that the kid was the reason she'd left school. But the idea that the kid would grow up to be someone he would date…what were the odds?

Michael messaged her back asking for more details, but Traci answered that she'd rather discuss it in person. Michael then tried to reach Ziggy, texting and calling him. But he got no response.

The combination of waiting for Traci and not hearing back from Ziggy had made the last day torturous. He was so full of anxiety about the situation that all he could do was stay in bed, drink straight vodka, and binge watch Beyoncé videos.

While waiting in the restaurant for Traci, Michael came up with a number of different theories about what Traci had to tell him. Maybe Ziggy had a terminal disease. Maybe he was criminally insane. Almost anything seemed plausible at this point.

Michael glanced at his phone to check the time. It was 10:35 a.m., five minutes after they were supposed to meet. A waitress, who resembled a less drug addled Amy Winehouse, came over and asked if he was ready to order.

"I'm still waiting on someone," Michael said.

"I'll be back," she replied.

As she walked away, Michael saw a short woman with a stylishly frizzy 'fro rush through the door. It was instantly clear to him that it was Traci, even though her hair was shorter and her face fuller. Despite all the anxiety he felt, he couldn't help but smile at the sight of his old friend.

He stood up and greeted her with a hug.

"Wow, it's been such a long time," he said.

"Yeah," she answered nervously, removing her leather jacket and placing it on the back of her chair.

"Weird circumstances, right?" Michael said, sitting back down.

"You could say that."

"I have so many questions," Michael said. "Ziggy is your son? You're his mom? That doesn't even seem possible. How did you know we knew each other?"

"Facebook. Isn't that how anyone knows anything these days?"

"I guess."

"I saw that you two were, um, 'in a relationship'."

Michael blushed.

"Um, yeah," Michael said, looking down into his napkin "I mean, I know it seems weird, the age difference and all. I'm a lot older, obviously. I mean, you know how old I am. And, of course, you know how old Ziggy is since he's your—"

"Michael, I'm not here to judge the situation," Traci said. "Do I think it's weird? Yes. Does it bother me? Yes. I'm not going to lie. But there's more going on."

"More? Like what? And why won't Ziggy return my calls?"

"He's very angry." Lines formed on Traci's forehead.

"Angry? Angry at what?" Michael said.

"At the whole situation. Like I said, I need to explain some things."

The waitress came back over.

"Coffee, ma'am?" she asked.

"Yes, please."

The waitress filled an empty coffee cup on the table.

"Are you ready to order?" she asked.

"No. Can you give me a moment?" Traci said, looking over the plastic menu. Michael felt like she was stalling.

"Is there something you'd recommend?" she asked Michael.

He started to say, "I recommend that you fucking tell me what you came here to tell me." But he caught himself.

"All the omelets are good," he said.

"Yeah, I remember you used to love omelets. I remember how we would come home from clubbing and stay up until the dining hall opened so we could hit up the omelette bar."

"Traci, I don't mean to be rude. And I'd love to reminisce sometime. But I've got to know what you came to all this way to tell me. It's driving me nuts."

Traci took a deep breath. "It's just very hard to say. It has to do with—"

"Are you ready to order now?" The waitress asked, seeming to appear from nowhere. Michael and Traci both jumped.

"I'll take the Wonderland omelette, with potatoes, no toast," said Traci.

"And what will you be having, sir?" the waitress asked Michael.

"The Eau Claire. Same thing, potatoes, no toast."

"I'll have that right out for you" the waitress said. She rushed off as quickly as she appeared.

"I forgot what I was saying." Traci said.

"You were starting to tell me whatever was is you needed to tell me."

"Yes. And I know that you're dying to know. But I think it's important that you have the context, so that you understand the decisions that I felt I had to make at the time."

"Please just tell me already," Michael said.

"Do you remember the night that we spent together, that we slept together?"

"The sex night," Michael said. "Yeah, you tend remember losing your cherry. That was my first time, boy or girl."

"Right. It just started happening and I sort of let it continue to happen."

"What's the big deal? That was nearly 20 years ago."

"The big deal is that I got pregnant. I got pregnant that night."

"What?"

"Ziggy is your son," Traci said.

"More coffee?" The waitress returned to the table, silver carafe in hand.

"What?" said Michael.

"I asked if you'd like more coffee, sir," said the waitress.

"No. I was saying 'what' to her, not you."

"Well, *would* you like more coffee, sir?" the waitress asked.

"No," Michael said. "Please, we're sort of in the middle of something."

The waitress rolled her eyes and walked away.

"That can't be true," Michael said. "We barely did anything."

"I know." Traci shrugged her shoulders.

"You told me you got pregnant by some teacher, some married professor or something."

"That's what I told everyone."

"Why would you lie?"

Traci shook her head and briefly closed her eyes.

"I can tell you why. But I know that the answer won't make sense in terms of who we are today. But that was a long time ago."

"How could you not have told me?" Michael asked.

Traci put down her coffee. "Do you remember what you said when I told you I was pregnant?"

"No."

"It was something on the order of 'sucks for you.'"

"I did not."

"You did."

"I was 19."

"Do you remember what you said next?"

"No, but I suppose you do," Michael said.

"You were like, 'I guess you have to get rid of it.' And then you offered to go with me to the abortion clinic, so you could be, as you said 'like the supportive friend in an Afterschool special.'"

"I was just trying to lighten the mood," Michael said. "I didn't know what to say. I felt bad for you. I felt bad that something so heavy happened to you. I wanted it to be over with so things could go back to the way they were. But then you decided to keep the baby. And, I don't know, I didn't understand why, like I couldn't relate to what you were doing."

"Exactly," Traci said. "The idea of telling you that the baby was yours was inconceivable. You were a child. We both were. But I was ready, or at least willing, to grow up. You were still figuring it out."

The waitress came back and laid plates in front of both of them. She again rolled her eyes at Michael as she walked away.

"How could you keep this from me for so long?" Michael said. "It's fucking unbelievable."

"I don't know, Michael. I don't have a good answer. It's not like I thought it out in advance. I suppose I planned on telling you one day. But you know, life happens…" She cut off a piece of her omelette.

"Does Ziggy know?"

"He does now."

"How did he take it?"

Traci finished chewing. "I guess the fact that he hasn't committed matricide suggests that he's taking it about as well as can be expected."

"But you told him that he had a sperm donor. He had a whole bit about it. That is such a betrayal."

"It's not!" Traci dropped her fork with a clank. "You can't *betray* an infant. Everything you do when you become a parent is to protect your child. That's what I was doing. I thought it would be better for him to think he didn't have a father than to have a father who wasn't ready for him, who would always be this weird absence in his life."

"But you didn't give me a choice."

"I didn't feel like I could take that chance." Traci said.

"I want to talk to Ziggy." Michael demanded.

"He doesn't want to talk to you."

"Why? I didn't fucking do anything."

"He said he isn't ready. He wanted me to ask you to stop calling and texting him."

"Oh, so suddenly I'm the asshole?"

"I think…I suspect he's just really embarrassed about everything that went on between you two," Traci said. She stared down into her plate, then looked up. "I mean, did you actually—

"

"Fuck?" Michael said.

Terror flashed on Traci's face.

"None of your fucking business," Michael said as cruelly as he could.

Traci's bottom lip trembled.

"But, no," Michael quickly admitted. He always found it so exhausting to be mean. "We never actually had sex."

Traci exhaled sharply. Then she made an eye wiping gesture with her fingers that made Michael think she might start to cry. After a few moments, she looked up and said, "I really don't know what to say about all of this. I did what I did because I thought it was the right thing to do. I did the best that I could do at the time. I wish I could tell you that I would change things if I could do them over again. But I know I wouldn't. That's the truth. And I really don't know what else to say. It seems superficial to say I'm sorry…"

"It's a fucking start."

"What?" Traci asked.

"It's a start to say, 'I'm sorry.'"

"Michael," Traci said. "I'm sorry."

Chapter 17

Once brunch was over, Michael stood on the corner and watched as Traci pulled out of a parking space and headed down Wickenden Street. He stood there while an older woman with frizzy red hair and glasses walked a bulldog past him. Minutes later, Michael was still there when a slightly rusting Toyota pulled into the space and two nerdy guys got out talking loudly and animatedly about the gender politics of *Game of Thrones*. A few minutes after that, the old woman with the bulldog walked back by holding a cup of coffee. She eyed Michael suspiciously. The bulldog let out a little growl. Michael felt it best to move.

The problem was that Michael didn't know where to go. The last thing he wanted to do was go home and be by himself. He needed to talk. He felt like it was the only way to detangle the jumble of thoughts that were rapidly expanding in his head like some kind of brain ramen.

He called Sidney, but there was no answer. He'd been trying to reach Sidney since the night Ziggy stormed out of his apartment, but to no avail. This was extremely strange since they generally touched base everyday with few exceptions. Under normal circumstances, Michael would be concerned. But these weren't normal circumstances, and he couldn't handle another worry.

Michael started walking up Wickenden. He knew where he was headed, but he wasn't ready to admit it to himself. He didn't want to face the possibility of rejection. He wouldn't have wanted to face the fact that he had nowhere else to go.

He walked another block or so and turned off of Wickenden. Soon he was standing in front of Bruce's house. He hadn't spoken to Bruce since their argument a few weeks back.

He still wasn't sure what the fight had been about, but it didn't matter now.

Michael walked to the side entrance, opened the screen, and knocked three times on the door. He listened closely, but didn't hear any movement from inside. He turned to his right and saw some kid racing down the street on his bike. He looked back toward the door and thought he could make out some sounds, like the loud thump of feet clomping down stairs. Michael saw the white curtain on the door draw back briefly, then heard multiple clanks from locks being undone. The door creaked open to reveal the towering figure of Bruce in white boxers and a wife beater. His face seemed to say, "What the fuck are you doing here?" But instead he said, "I buy my Girl Scout shit at the office."

Michael tried to smile, but it came across more like a grimace. "You still mad?" Michael asked.

"I don't know what the fuck I am."

Bruce threw the door open a little wider and walked back inside. Michael followed him to the living room. A Nascar race played on the flatscreen.

"Do we need to, like, clear the air or something?" Michael asked. "The last time I saw you, you were super-pissed."

"I don't want to get all into it again," Bruce said, putting down his can of Bud Light. "I was pissed that you lied to me or didn't tell me about the guy you were dating…whatever. I don't like not knowing shit."

"I'm sorry."

Bruce said: "It just seems like, more and more, random shit gets thrown my way. There's so much in life that you can't plan for."

"You can say that again," Michael said.

"So, are you still seeing that guy?" Bruce picked up his beer again and took a long pull.

"Not exactly."

"What do you mean?"

"Hey, do you have another beer?" Michael asked.

"You don't drink beer."

"Do you have vodka?"

"It's 11 a.m."

"So, mix it with orange juice or some shit."

"Jesus!" Bruce got up and walked into the kitchen.

Michael stared at the TV without really watching. He realized that once he told Bruce about Ziggy, the whole thing would be real. It would force him out of the feeling that he was lost in some alternative comic book universe.

"I'm out of OJ," Bruce yelled from the kitchen.

"Got any Quik?"

"Strawberry or chocolate?"

"Strawberry. And make it strong."

A few moments later, Bruce walked back in the room carrying a tall ice-filled glass with a mass of pink liquid at the top and about two inches of clear fluid at the bottom. "You realize this is, like, the grossest shit ever, right?" Bruce said.

"Fuck you. I used to drink it all the time in college. It's called a Wacky Wabbit."

Bruce laughed. "You're making that shit up."

"Fuckin' am not." Michael stirred the drink with his finger and then he took a gulp.

"So, why won't you tell me if you're still seeing that guy? First, you didn't tell me you were seeing him and now—"

"It's not that I won't tell you." Michael took another swig from his drink. "It's just that shit has gotten insanely complicated."

"Complicated how?"

"I just found out the craziest shit about him, about us."

"What?" Bruce's eyes widened and his mouth made a hungry smirk.

"I'm gonna tell you. I gotta tell someone. But here's the thing, a very important thing."

"What?"

"You can not laugh."

"I'm not gonna fuckin' laugh."

"I mean, I understand how the situation could seem funny on some level. But it's not funny, not to me. It's totally fucked me up and I need you to take it seriously."

"What the fuck is it? Shit!"

"I don't even know how to fucking say it."

"Just fuckin' say it!"

"O.K., here goes." Michael took another long sip. "I just found out, like just now at breakfast, that the guy I've been seeing is kinda my son."

"What?" Bruce's mouth sprayed beer in every direction. "How is that even possible?"

"I have to fucking tell you where babies come from?" Michael said, wiping some of Bruce's beer from his face. "One night in college, I hooked up with a friend, a 'girl' friend, my best friend at the time, and she got pregnant. But I didn't know the baby was mine. She told me that she got pregnant from some married professor she was having a fling with. I believed her, never gave it another thought. Anyway, she left school, had the baby. We lost touch. Cut to 19 year later. The kids going to RISD and I'm dating him. Or I was."

"Oh shit, did you guys fuck?"

"Why does everyone keep asking that?"

"'Cause it's gross."

"No, we didn't fuck. Almost, but thankfully not."

"That is so fucking unbelievable. How did you find out?"

"His mom saw that we were in a relationship on Facebook. She met me this morning to explain the whole shit."

"No wonder you looked so spooked when you got here."

"Is that why you let me in?"

"I don't know. I can't really stay mad at people. It's one of my faults."

"I'll remember that." Michael said.

"What are you gonna do now?"

"I don't fuckin' know. Ziggy won't talk to me. He won't return my calls. It's like he thinks I did something wrong."

"Well, look on the bright side," Bruce said. "At least you won't have to waste a lot of time wondering if your kid is gonna grow up to be a queer."

Michael took a pillow from the couch and aimed it square at Bruce's laughing face.

"Hey," Bruce said, as the pillow hit him; some beer spilled on his shirt.

As Michael watched Bruce rub the wet spots on his tank top, he thought he heard footsteps coming down the stairs. Then it sounded as if someone had entered the kitchen and was opening up drawers.

"Who's that?" Michael mouthed, pointing toward the kitchen.

"Fuck!" Bruce said. "I guess there's something I gotta tell you too."

"What?"

"My ma," Bruce whisper-talked. "She's kinda been living with me."

"Why? What's up?"

Bruce leaned closer to Michael so that he could talk quietly. "The thing is, she's sick. It's the Alzheimers. Well, Alzheimer's Disease."

"Oh, shit!" Michael said, looking grave.

"It's not as bad as all that." Bruce said. "Well, it can be. She has good and bad days. But the bottom line is she can't really be alone no more, so I moved her in with me."

"Why didn't you tell anyone?"

"'Cause I didn't want to be that sad middle-aged homo who's taking care of his sick mother. Noone wants to fuck *that* guy."

"Bruce?" a woman called from the kitchen.

"Let me introduce you," Bruce said. He got up and started toward the kitchen. Michael followed him. There was a small woman in a buttoned-down white shirt and faded jeans with an apron around her waist. She wore her gray hair pulled back into a bun, and her face was bold like Bruce's, only softer.

"Ma," Bruce said. "This is Michael, my friend."

Chapter 18

Sidney awoke, sluggishly, perhaps druggedly, as his
surroundings slowly came into focus. The first thing he noticed
was the bed he was in. It was about a third of the size of the one
he had at home. His legs felt thick and heavy, tucked beneath
scratchy, white sheets and a thin, cotton blanket the color of
oatmeal.

Sidney looked to his left. Several tubes, anchored by
clear tape, stuck out from his arms, connecting him to various
bags of fluid and a machine with digitized numbers. A feeling
came over him like he'd suddenly remembered something he had

forgotten. He thought, "I'm in the hospital." He'd been there for days.

He looked up from the bed. Playing on the wall-mounted TV was an episode of *Good Times*. Sidney always watched old sitcoms when he wasn't feeling well. Sometimes, he could go for days watching nothing but TV reruns from the '50s, '60s, and '70s. But sooner or later, he'd snap out of it after seeing one too many commercials for stair lifts and AARP-approved Medicare supplement plans.

Sidney reached for his phone on the table next to him. There were several messages from Michael, but that was about it. Two days earlier, as he'd sat in the emergency room, he'd texted his assistant: "Won't be in for a few days. Need to take care of some stuff. Will explain ltr." The moment he pressed send, he thought how strange it would be if that was the last text he ever wrote.

The whole incident started two days earlier as he was leaving work. He hadn't felt right all day, but he wasn't able to pinpoint exactly what was wrong. He felt achy, irritable, and mildly bloated. Sometimes when he was under the weather, he'd get so caught up in his work that he'd forget he was feeling bad. But not that day. No matter what he tried—Advil, Tums, Starbucks—he just couldn't shake the malaise.

Sidney stopped by Whole Foods on the way home. He knew it was ridiculous, but on some level, he thought that if he ate some organic food when he was starting to feel bad, he could ward off whatever was coming. He got a grilled pasture-raised chicken breast from the deli and then went to the salad bar. But each step felt like he was walking in sand. Once he got to the salad bar, it took great effort just to lift the empty salad container.

At this point, he got nervous. Sweat flash-flooded from his forehead, under his arms, and his crotch. He needed to get out of there. He didn't think he had the strength to stand in line. He tucked the wrapped chicken breast into a sparsely populated rack of *Vanity Fair*s and headed home.

By the time he got to his apartment, he felt like his whole body was racing to come undone. He fell onto the couch and tried to slow his breathing. It didn't work. His heart seemed like it was simultaneously working too hard and not hard enough. He knew then that he needed to go to the hospital. For a moment, he thought about calling Michael, but Michael was so excitable, and Sidney couldn't afford to expend any energy calming him down.

As he lay on the couch, Sidney realized that this was the moment people had been telling him to prepare for his entire life. Whenever Sidney conversationally pooh-poohed the idea of needing some kind of "life partner," the other person would come back with something on the order of, "who's going to take care of you when you're sick." The presumptive "when" always annoyed Sidney. At that moment, though, aching and alone on the couch, Sidney felt almost a sense of vindication, because what he wanted most wasn't some abstract caregiver, just any old "who" that he happened to be with in order to stave off loneliness and the need for a wearable medical alert device. What he wanted, in fact, was a very specific, tangible person. He wanted Dante. He wanted him on the couch beside him, holding his hand, reassuring him by his very presence that everything would be all right.

But that wasn't possible. He had no idea where Dante was. Dante had removed his ad from RentMe and his old cell number no longer worked. Sidney had tried it about a week earlier just to see. He'd been prepared to explain the call as a "butt dial," but there was no answer.

Sidney's heart started racing again. He knew he had to go to the hospital, but how would he get there? An ambulance seemed gauche. Instead he decided to Über. That was more discreet.

Sidney tossed some toiletries and underwear in a Louis Vuitton overnight bag and made his way out the door. At the elevator, he remembered that he'd forgotten his iPad. He was about to turn back for it, when he was struck with a stab of pain in his left shoulder. He knew then that time was of the essence. The elevator opened and he got in.

The next 48 hours brought a dizzying rush of tests. He didn't recall most of it, but he did distinctly remember being questioned by a black female nurse shortly after arriving at the hospital. She'd asked if he'd ever seen a cardiologist before, and he said no. Then she asked if he had a family history of heart disease.

"My father," Sidney said.

The nurse looked at Sidney as if to say, "and…"

"He, um, died of a heart attack," Sidney continued. He glanced up at the nurse expecting sympathy. But instead, she flashed him a side-eye look that seemed to say: "Negro, you know your ass should've gotten your heart checked a long time ago."

Once admitted to the hospital, the doctors decided that he didn't need surgery, not right away at least. But they kept him for what was sure to be an expensive bout of observation. He spent a lot of time in bed thinking about his father, who died when he was a toddler. Sidney realized that he'd always just thought of his father as "gone." But he had once been "here." Sidney was proof of that. Why had he given so little thought to his father's life? Why had he given so little thought to the idea that his own life would one day end?

Sidney's thoughts then turned to Dante. He wondered if he made a mistake by not dating him. In fact, he knew he'd made a mistake. But he also knew that it was the only decision he could've made at the time. The idea of being alone had become almost like religion for him; he'd committed to it mind, body, and soul. He hadn't wanted to put himself in the position of needing anyone for any reason. He'd only wanted things in his life that he could be sure of, that he had some degree of control over. But now he realized that life only came with one true certainty. It is a limited engagement.

Part Six

Chapter 19

Michael was looking through old photos on his laptop, when his phone buzzed with a message from Bruce: "What are we doing tonight?" Reading it, Michael felt that the "we" was somehow italicized: "What are *we* doing tonight?" This made him realize, perhaps for the first time, how much his relationship with Bruce had changed over the past couple of weeks.

Michael and Bruce had spent nearly every night together since the day Michael went over to Bruce's house after his brunch with Traci. But whatever they were doing still felt casual and off the cuff. Michael would text Bruce asking him what he was doing for dinner. Bruce would tell Michael to come by to watch TV and have a drink. Then they would almost always have sex. But neither Michael nor Bruce had acknowledged the frequency of what they were doing nor had they explored the idea that it might mean something different, something deeper perhaps than their 911-emergency hook-ups of the past. This was why Bruce's text seemed like such a game changer. It made them a "we."

Michael put the phone down on the table and slumped in his chair. He didn't know exactly how he felt about this "we"-ness. He didn't really want to think about it. Ever since learning the news about Ziggy, he'd only wanted to do things that didn't require much thought or reflection. Hanging out with Bruce had fulfilled this need. But this text forced him to think about shit again. It was as if he'd been hiding under covers and someone had just snatched them off.

Michael picked up his phone and typed: "I might go to Mirror Ball." He wished there some way he could italicize the "I." But before he pressed send, he opted for something softer and more inclusive: "Wanna go to Mirror Ball?"

Michael hadn't been to the Mirror Ball since all of the stuff with Ziggy went down. Michael deeply wanted to talk to Ziggy, if just to see how he was. But running into him at the Mirror Ball didn't seem to be the right way to go about it. But at this point, Michael was starting to feel like a prisoner in a town that had less than a handful of gay clubs. He knew he'd wind up going to the Mirror Ball sooner or later. It might as well be tonight.

His phone buzzed with a new text from Bruce: "Pick you up at 11."

Michael and Bruce walked into the Mirror Ball and went straight to the top floor. Michael knew that if Ziggy was there, he'd likely be downstairs. The top floor was surprisingly crowded, but they found one empty table in the corner.

"I'm gonna get us drinks," Bruce said and headed toward the bar. Michael's mind stuck on Bruce's use of "us." Had he used "us" when he got them drinks in the past or was this something different? Michael knew he was reading too much into everything, but he couldn't help it.

"Here ya go, honey," Bruce said a few minutes later, handing Michael his drink.

"What?" Michael said, nearly squealing.

"I'm joking," Bruce laughed.

"I know that," Michael said, lowering his voice.

"Then why'd you jump out of your skin?"

"I didn't jump out of my skin. I just didn't hear you."

"O.K., sweetheart," Bruce said, laughing again.

Michael was about to tell him to shut up, when an older pauchy man came over and tapped Bruce on the shoulder.

"Hey, stranger," the man said. "Sorry to interrupt, but it's been so long since I've seen you."

Bruce greeted and firmly hugged the man, who Michael didn't know but had seen around. The man kept complimenting Bruce on how good he looked as his hands grazed Bruce's arms and shoulders. While this was going on, Michael's attention started to wander. He surveyed the room and spotted his ex Jimmy sitting at the bar with his new boyfriend.

Michael watched them for a while. He couldn't really see their faces, but he could tell how they felt about each other. They looked like people in love, a couple. It was the way their bodies swayed toward each other as they talked. It was like a dance. Michael wondered if he had ever looked like that with someone? He wondered what he and Bruce looked like together? Would an outside observer think they were in a relationship? Were they in a relationship? Should they be in one? Perhaps he had feelings for Bruce that he wasn't ready to admit. Perhaps he was the dude who doth protest too much.

Michael had completely finished his drink and was using the straw to play around with his ice by the time the man talking to Bruce finally left.

"How do you know him?" Michael asked.

"Oh, I just know him from around. He's a cop queen—you know, a guy who's into cops."

Michael nodded.

"A po-po ho," Bruce continued. "That's what they call us in the hood, you know, po-po."

Michael rolled his eyes. "Yeah. I'm black."

"Yeah, but you're…what is it Sidney calls you? Boogie?"

"Bourgie."

"Yeah, bourgie. It means you grew up more *Cosby* than *Good Times*, right? More *Family Matters* than *What's Happening*, more *Boondocks* than *Fat Albert*, more…"

"Shut up!" Michael yelled.

"Jesus, what crawled up your fuck-hole?"

"Nothing. You're being annoying."

"You're in a bad fucking mood."

"I'm not in a bad mood. I just have shit on my mind."

"Like what?"

"Like nothing," Michael said. "Like everything! Like all the obvious shit. I probably shouldn't have come out tonight."

Bruce was quiet for a moment. Then he smiled and touched one of Michael's hands, "I'm glad you did."

They each had another drink. Michael slowly relaxed. It was a feeling not unlike releasing your stomach after a period of holding it in. He continued to watch Jimmy and his boyfriend interact at the bar. Strangely, he wasn't jealous. He was happy that Jimmy had found something good.

About a half hour later, Michael and Bruce were getting ready to go, when Michael saw Jimmy's boyfriend head toward the restroom. "I want to say hi to Jimmy for a second," Michael said. Bruce told him that he would go get the car and wait outside. Michael took a last sip from his drink and walked to the bar. Jimmy had his back turned and was saying something to the bartender. The bartender spotted Michael and gave Jimmy an "uh oh" look. Jimmy turned around.

"Uh, hey," Michael said.

"Hey," Jimmy answered, unenthusiastically.

"How goes stuff?" Michael asked.

"Good. Things are really good."

"I see that you're out with your guy."

"Yeah, we're sorta celebrating," Jimmy said. "We signed a lease today. We're moving in together."

"Wow," Michael said. "That's really awesome for you. I mean, I know that's what you wanted, the whole living together thing."

"Yeah, it's cool."

"I just wanted to let you to know that I was sitting here watching you guys, not like a stalker or anything. But I just wanted to say that you guys look good together, and you seem happy. And I guess I wanted to say that I'm happy for you. I know I'm supposed to say that, but it's actually true. I'm happy for you."

"Thanks," Jimmy said, his lips curling into a smile. "That means a lot."

"I guess you have to say that too, huh?" Michael said.

Jimmy touched Michael's arm. "No, I mean it."

Michael hugged Jimmy goodbye and headed downstairs. He was about to walk outside, but decided to go to the restroom first. It felt like all the vodka he'd been drinking had gone straight to the head of his dick. Michael opened the bathroom door. Standing at the sink, splashing water on his face, was Ziggy.

The first thing Michael noticed was that Ziggy had cut off his mohawk. He now sported a marine-like, high-and-tight crew cut. The second thing Michael noticed was how the entire bathroom reeked of freshly spewed puke. Ziggy wavered

slightly, like a sapling in a breeze before steadying himself at the

sink.

"Are you O.K.?" Michael asked.

"What the fuck are you doing here?" Ziggy spat.

Well, I was trying to pee, but…"

Ziggy's eyes closed drowsily, then snapped open

quickly.

"Have you been drinking?" Michael asked.

"Fuck you. You're not my…" Ziggy kicked the wall

with his Doc Martens. "Fuck!"

"You know, we really should talk about all this."

"I don't want to talk about anything."

"I know it's awkward, but…"

"But nothing." Ziggy kicked the wall again.

"Why are you so mad at me? I didn't keep anything

from you. I didn't know."

"It doesn't matter that you didn't know," Ziggy said,

gaining a modicum of sobriety through his rage. "You're such a

fucking flake that my mom didn't even want me to know about

you. She didn't want me to know that you existed. She thought you were *that* fucked up, that much of a loser. She didn't want you to fuck up my life. But you ended up fucking it up anyway. Seriously, it was better not having a dad than learning that my dad is such a sad, fucking loser."

"That's really unfair."

"I don't care what you think is fair. Just fucking leave me alone. Stop texting me. Stop calling me..."

Ziggy swayed again. He grabbed for the sink and nearly missed it. Michael reached for Ziggy's shoulder.

"Touch me and die," Ziggy said. He wiped his mouth with the back of his hand and staggered out of the bathroom. Michael stared at the back of the door for a moment and then walked into a stall. He tried to pee but his hands were shaking too much.

He left the restroom and dazedly walked through the crowd, not speaking or meeting anyone's eyes. He made his way outside where Bruce sat in the driver's seat of his pickup, looking at his watch.

"What the fuck took so long?" Bruce asked.

Michael didn't answer. He just said "let's go home," and he didn't care where Bruce took him.

Chapter 20

Ziggy stood on the edge of a parking lot rooftop, bathed in a yellowish glow from the overhead lights. He loved the look of an empty parking garage. There was something about the concrete barrenness that moved him.

Ziggy walked along the ledge of the building, woozy from all he'd been drinking earlier. He took another step along the ledge, but this time he let one foot slip over the side of the building. He closed his eyes, took a breath and made a short jump in the air. For a moment, he didn't know if he was going to land with both feet on the edge or go plunging three stories below. The feeling didn't scare him, though. What he felt was freeing, a release from everything on his mind. When he landed a few seconds later and felt the ledge beneath his feet, he opened his eyes and smiled.

Ziggy discovered this parking lot during his first week at school when he'd set off by himself to explore the city. After that, he'd go there from time to time to clear his head. He'd been coming a lot more since he got the news about his mom and Michael.

When his mom explained the whole story over dinner, Ziggy felt like he needed to hold himself back, almost the way a trainer would bridle a horse. His anger felt like a separate entity that was ready to burst from inside him.

After dinner, Ziggy's mom told him that she was having brunch with Michael the next day.

"What do you want me to tell him?" she asked.

"To leave me the fuck alone," he said.

As he said it, he knew that part of him wanted to say the same thing to her. But he couldn't. He couldn't hurt his mother like that. So he chose the next best target.

In the weeks that followed, his mom kept trying to talk about the issue, calling almost daily and asking if he was alright. Ziggy never answered. The one thing he knew for sure was that he didn't want to talk about it. He didn't want to talk about anything. Finally, his mother texted him: "Just let me you're alive." He texted back: "Not dead."

Ziggy was just so angry, more than he'd ever been in life. There were so many fucked up things about the situation, not least of which was the barf-worthy creepiness of almost getting butt-fucked by his dad. But the thing that made him most angry was the idea that he had let himself be duped all of those years. Why hadn't he figured it out before?

In retrospect, none of his mom's stories made sense. Why would a 19-year-old get artificially inseminated? There would've been legions of dudes willing to sperm-up for free? Besides, where would an unemployed college student have gotten the money for such a procedure? He couldn't believe that he'd never questioned these things before.

In many ways, it reminded him of when he was 6 and some older kids told him that there was no Santa Claus. At first, the revelation was shocking. But once it was all explained to him, he couldn't understand how he'd ever fallen for it in the first place. How could some guy make all these toys, fly around the world delivering them, and then squeeze his fat ass down a multitude of chimneys? The apartment where Ziggy then lived didn't even have a chimney.

A couple of days after that revelation, Ziggy's mom took him to see Santa Claus at Wheaton Mall. He hadn't yet told her what he'd learned about the North Pole's most famous resident. While in line, his mom smiled and asked Ziggy what he was going to ask Santa, but Ziggy stayed silent and glared at Santa with contempt.

Once he was on Santa's lap, the Mall Claus asked what Ziggy wanted for Christmas. Ziggy answered, "nothin'." Santa asked if Ziggy had been a good boy that year, and Ziggy said, "none of your business." Then Ziggy balled his small hands into fists and leapt off Santa's lap by pounding his hands into Santa's groin. Ziggy wanted to hurt him for being a phony.

Mall Claus gasped for air and make a sound that was something like "oooolph." Traci was horrified. She ordered Ziggy to apologize.

"Sorry," Ziggy said, eyes toward the ground. He did feel bad about it. He'd wanted to hurt the man, but he didn't want the man to actually be hurt.

Mall Claus laughed it off as best he could, saying something on the order of "boys will be boys." Traci thanked Santa, apologized again, and added, with a bit of shakiness in her voice, "Merry Christmas."

When Traci and Ziggy were back in their car, Traci yelled, "Why did you do that?"

"'Cause he's not Santa," Ziggy said. "It's a lie!"

"How do you know that?"

"Some big kids told me. There is no Santa. Why did you lie to me?"

"Because it's fun," Traci said, shrilly. "Santa Claus is fun. I believed in Santa when I was little. Everyone believes in Santa. I was just trying to make you happy."

"It doesn't make me happy when you lie," Ziggy said.

Traci started the car, and they rode home in silence.

Recalling this incident, Ziggy felt himself getting colder. He wondered for a moment if he was somehow internalizing this winter memory. But then a chilly wind laced with beads of rain slapped him in the face. He continued walking along the ledge of the parking lot.

He was almost ready to go back to his dorm, but not just yet. He took a few more steps on the newly slick surface. Once again, he let his foot drop over the edge of the building. He closed his eyes and hopped into the air. There was that welcome feeling of surrender. His feet landed on the ledge, but this time something was different. The surface below his shoes was wet. He wasn't able to steady himself. He started falling. His body jerked backward and his right leg shot back over the side of the building. His stomach tightened with fear. His left arm extended reflexively and he grabbed the wet ledge as tightly as he could. The concrete scraped his skin, but he held on. He breathed deeply and brought his right leg back onto the other side of the ledge. He took another deep breath and sat down on the garage

floor. As the fear drained from his body, he smiled.

Chapter 21

Sidney arrived at Whole Foods around five in the
evening. Ever since the heart scare, going to Whole Foods was a
daily health conscious ritual for him. He'd even taken on the
arrogance of a frequent shopper. He'd become annoyed when
someone took too much time browsing in the aisles, like how
could one not already know their preference for a particular
brand of organic stone ground mustard? Today he had to catch
himself from confronting a child who had the audacity to take a
Emmentaler cheese sample without using tongs.

But it wasn't just ill mannered children that were on his
mind. A conversation with Michael earlier that day had left him

unsettled. Michael had stopped by the gallery to sign a print, and this gave them the chance to finally catch up. Sidney came clean about his hospital stay, and Michael overreacted expectedly.

"How could you not tell me?" Michael said, nearly worked up to tears.

"Michael, it wasn't about you, for Christ's sake. It was my heart attack or, rather, my near heart attack. My heart scare, so to speak. And I didn't want anyone to know."

"But why?"

"Because! Because…I don't know. The whole thing felt so stupid. It seemed so ridiculous that it all could've ended like that, alone in the emergency room, sitting on a hard ass plastic chair watching an evening replay of *The Wendy Williams Show*. I didn't want anyone to see me in that state, not even you."

"But you know I'm here for you, right?"

"Yes, dear, I know. But sometimes you don't want to *need* people. You don't want have reached the age of shit breaking down and going bad. You don't want to admit it to yourself, and you damn sure don't want witnesses."

For several minutes, they talked about Sidney's illness, the various medications he was taking, and his resolve to live healthier. The conversation then moved to recent events of Michael's life. Michael had already told Sidney about Ziggy being his son, but he hadn't brought him up to speed with what was going on Bruce.

"You guys are dating now?" Sidney asked. "Like official?"

"I don't know what we're doing," Michael said. "I mean, I know what we're doing, but I don't know what it means."

Sidney smiled and raised an eyebrow. "What do you want it mean?"

"I don't fuckin' know," Michael said, slumping in his chair. "It's been cool spending time with him. But looking down the road, I don't know what I want."

"What does he want?"

"I think he wants us to be, like, boyfriends. And I keep asking myself, "Do I want this? Should I want this?""

"Why do you have to decide?"

"Because he wants to know. He wants to know what we're doing. I'm seeing him later tonight. He's taking me out to eat. It's supposed to be our big let's-talk-about-shit dinner."

"What are you going to say?"

"I have no fucking idea."

"Just say you need time to think about it?" Sidney offered.

"That's what I've been saying."

"And how does he respond?"

"'Think yes.' He says, 'Michael, I want you to think yes." Michael looked at Sidney. "What do you think I should do?"

For one of the first times in his life, Sidney didn't have an answer.

This conversation stayed with Sidney, as he made his way through Whole Foods. He was irked that he hadn't known how to advise Michael. Sidney hated indecisiveness. It was so plebeian. But Sidney knew why the answer to Michael's question had eluded him. When Dante had asked Sidney to essentially "think yes" regarding their relationship, he hadn't been able to do it. He hadn't been able to conceive of doing it, of trusting someone with the task of loving him. The idea of a relationship with Dante was so outside the realm of what he'd come to expect for his life that he couldn't process it. He'd never imagined that happiness could come so easily. He'd just assumed that fate was serving him a cruel ruse.

But in the weeks since he left the hospital, Sidney had gained new insights about the situation. He knew without a doubt that he'd made a mistake in rejecting Dante. He should've told him yes. He should've given happiness a shot. He now wondered—more soberly than sadly—if he would regret this decision for the rest of his waking days.

Sidney finished shopping and headed to his BMW convertible with a dinner of herb-roasted rotisserie chicken and steamed string beans. Sidney started the car and headed toward the main exit, but he saw that it was backed up with a long line of cars waiting to merge onto the Main St. thoroughfare. Sidney huffed, but tried to stay calm. He made a sharp turn to go around the back of the building toward a less-trafficked side exit. He thought he was in the clear until he saw a large red pickup truck parked at the Whole Foods receiving dock. The space behind the store was very narrow, and the truck was situated in such a way that Sidney couldn't get past it.

"Now ain't that some shit," Sidney thought as he stepped on the brake.

He let out another huff and fiddled with the radio, catching the tail end of a Chaka Khan song on the R&B oldies station. He looked ahead and saw no signs of life anywhere near the truck. There was no one in the cab, on the dock, or behind the truck. He was about to pound the horn, when he spotted a young man in a baseball cap walk from the back of Whole Foods. The guy got into the driver's seat of the truck.

Sidney put his car back into drive and waited for the truck to move. Then he saw something—someone—completely unexpected. At first, he doubted that what he was seeing was real. He thought he'd just conjured this figure based on all of the stuff he'd been thinking about earlier. But as the person grew nearer, walking from the back of Whole Foods into the passenger seat of the truck, Sidney realized that he was seeing the flesh-and-blood truth. It was Dante.

Sidney was so stunned by this turn of events that he didn't notice his car drifting forward ever so slightly, until it made contact with the side of the truck. The guy in the baseball hat jumped out.

"What the hell?" he yelled.

A flustered Sidney put his car into park and turned it off. "I'm so sorry," he said. "My foot must have slipped from the brake."

"You think?" the man said.

"Sidney?" said Dante, who had gotten out to see what was happening.

"You know him?" asked the man in the baseball cap.

"Yeah," Dante answered.

The driver shook his head as he inspected the side of the truck. "You're lucky that there doesn't seem to be any damage. I should make a report, but we need to..."

The man continued talking but Sidney didn't hear him. He was focused on Dante, watching Dante move toward him.

"Dude, where the fuck are you going?" shouted the driver. "We gotta get goin'. It's rush hour."

"O.K.," Dante called back. Then he said to Sidney, "good to see you."

"Yeah," said Sidney.

A clenched feeling took over Sidney's body. He had so much to say that it paralyzed him. He couldn't make a sound.

Dante watched Sidney expectantly, but after a few moments, his gaze dropped to the ground. He walked back to the truck. Soon afterward, the truck drove away.

As Sidney sat watching the truck pull out of the parking lot, a very distinct feeling hit him. It was similar to the sensation that you get just before jumping between closing elevator doors. He felt like he was being offered a tiny window of opportunity. He took it.

Sidney quickly started the car again and sped after the truck. At first, he didn't see it through all of the traffic. But then he spotted it in the distance, turning onto I-95. Sidney moved through the thick rush hour traffic as quickly as he could, but, by the time he merged onto the highway, the truck was out of sight.

Sidney's heart started beating fast, which he knew wasn't a good thing. There would be no point reuniting with Dante only to fall dead at his feet. That was not the kind of romantic gesture he wanted to make. Sidney forced himself to calm down. He took slow, deep breaths. In his mind, he heard Natalie Cole singing, "Que sera, sera."

Sidney continued driving down I-95 as fast as he could without bringing about an accident or another coronary event. He couldn't see the truck anywhere. Several exits went by and still no sign of it. He decided to drive one more mile before turning around and going home. He reset his odometer, and the numbers started moving quickly—06, 07, 08… Sidney moved into the far right lane. The odometer displayed a 1, and Sidney turned off at the next exit.

It put him on a two-lane road that didn't have any visible place to make a U-turn. He followed the road for a half-mile or so as it curved and curved through thick thatches of trees. A "Horse Crossing" sign told Sidney that he was far outside of his element.

Finally, after driving for another mile or so, he saw an intersection and a stoplight up ahead. He pressed heavy on the accelerator. He was anxious to put this whole stupid chase behind him. What had he been thinking? The light turned red just as Sidney arrived at the intersection. "Figures," Sidney thought. He looked around. The area was fairly barren except for a small wooden church to his right. Sidney read the placard outside the church: "If you see life through the eyes of faith, you will be surprised at what you see."

Sidney pondered this statement as he sat at the light. He had always placed his faith in his ability to overcome any obstacle, in his power to survive. But increasingly Sidney wondered if true faith meant daring to want something more than just survival, if true faith meant daring to dream.

The light turned green. Sidney was about to make a U-turn, but there was a cop stopped in the opposite direction. Sidney wasn't trying to get pulled over on some rural Rhode Island road with nobody else around. He knew all the risks of Driving-While-Black, not to mention Driving-A-Bimmer-While-Black.

He kept driving straight, past more fields of nothing. Then he saw, coming up on his left, a farm with a little corner store in front of it. Sidney turned into the parking area in front of the store which was covered in hand-painted signs for "Baked Pies," "Fresh Jams," and "Homemade Fudge." He thought about going inside to grab something sweet, but he'd been doing so well on his new healthy diet. He didn't want to break it now.

Sidney was pulling out of the parking lot when he noticed a smaller wooden building several feet behind the store. The building's door had a sign that read "Office." Parked beside the building was a red pickup truck. Was this the same truck? How could he find out? If it was the same truck, what should he do? What should he say?

A part of him wanted to rush to the office, but he knew that was foolish, not to mention potentially dangerous. He'd noticed more than a few "No Trespassing" signs around the property. Sidney decided to just wait. He parked his car so that he could see the truck and the office door.

About an hour passed. The sky grew darker, and Sidney had made it through his entire Sade's Greatest Hits playlist on

Spotify. Just when he thought that he probably should start heading back, the front door of the office opened, making a lemon yellow slice in the night. The guy with the baseball cap walked out of the door first, followed by Dante.

Sidney hopped out of his car and walked toward them.

"What the fuck?" said the guy in the baseball cap.

"It's O.K.," Dante told him.

"Can we talk?" Sidney asked Dante.

The truck driver, perhaps sensing an awkward situation, said, "I gotta take a piss. I'll be right back."

Dante nodded and walked toward Sidney. "What are you doing here?" Dante asked.

"I'm doing..." Sidney paused. "I'm doing what I should've done before. I need to tell you that I fucked up and that I want you. I want to be with you. I've always wanted to be with you. I just didn't have the guts, the balls, to say it before."

"I figured you just didn't want to be with me, like I was just some throwaway hustler to you."

"That was never it, never ever it. I'm so sorry if I made you feel that way. It was about me, all about me and how fucked up I am. But I'm very sorry, very very sorry. And if you come with me now, if we can talk, I will try to explain it to you better. If you give me another chance, I will do all that I can to make it up to you. I'll make it up to you for as long as you'll let me."

The guy in the baseball cap came back outside and walked to the truck.

"You comin'?" he asked Dante.

Dante turned to him, "No, I got a ride."

Part Seven

Chapter 22

Michael stood in his bathroom getting ready for his date

with Bruce. He still wasn't sure exactly what he was going to tell

him, whether he was going to "think yes." He'd tried all sorts of

strategies to come to a decision. He flipped a quarter that he'd

been saving for laundry, but he accidentally dropped it and it

rolled behind a bookcase.

Michael hated to admit it, but he knew that one of the

complicating factors of his decisions was Bruce's age. Michael

couldn't deny that he was mostly attracted to much younger

guys. Was that wrong? Was it wrong to want exactly what you

want?

At the same time, Michael sometimes wondered if there were any unfortunate side effects to his perpetual desire for younger guys, if his attraction to younger guys was in some ways a devaluation of himself.

About fifteen minutes later, Bruce picked Michael up outside of his house. Bruce gave him a tight hug, and Michael got a whiff of some alchemic combination of Speed Stick, Old Spice, and Irish Spring. Bruce seemed especially pulled together tonight. His shirt was pressed and tucked into a dark pair of jeans, and he wore a navy sports jacket. Michael felt a little underdressed in his faded knit polo from the boy's section of Target. But before he could get too self-conscious about it, Bruce told him, "You look nice."

They drove for several minutes until they got to Wayland Square. Michael had been so preoccupied with what he was going to tell Bruce that it hadn't dawned on him to ask where they were eating. Knowing Bruce, Michael just assumed it would involve steak. That was why he was so surprised when

Bruce parked the truck right in front of Michael's favorite sushi restaurant.

"I thought you hated sushi," Michael said. "I thought you hated all Japanese food."

"Yeah, well—"

"And Vietnamese food, and Chinese. I thought you were basically resistant to all 'ese' cuisine."

"Shut the fuck up. I'm trying new shit. You like it, right?"

"Yeah."

"O.K. then."

They entered the restaurant and a stylish female hostess in a satin dress led them to a small, dimly lit booth toward the back. They sat for several moments silently contemplating the menu. Michael's nerves increased with each passing moment. He still had no idea what he was going to tell Bruce.

The server came to the table, and Michael blurted out, "I'd like a cranberry sake-tini now. I mean, please."

"O.K.," said the server. "I guess that answers the question of whether or not you'd like something other than water to drink."

"I'll have the same thing," Bruce said.

"Do you even know what that is?" Michael asked.

"No, but whatever. I'll try it. How bad can it be? It has booze in it, right? "

Michael nodded. He didn't know if he should feel flattered by Bruce's restaurant choice and drink order or totally creeped out. He had never been seen Bruce try so hard to impress anyone, much less him.

Michael made it through drinks by keeping the conversation light. Earlier that day, a local politician had been caught in a gay sex scandal. Michael told Bruce how one local news show captioned the story: "Congressman caught in gay sex sandal."

"I definitely need a pair of those," Michael said.

Bruce laughed politely, but Michael could tell that he was slipping into a more serious mood.

When it came time to order, Michael got his favorite dish, a roll with spicy octopus, crab, cucumber, and an assortment of multi-colored fish eggs. Bruce ordered the chicken teriyaki platter. While they waited for their food, Michael found himself talking nonstop, saying anything to avoid actually having the talk. He knew that once they had that conversation, it would change things between them between them forever, for better or worse. Michael wasn't ready to cross that threshold, so he continued bringing up stuff that he had seen on TV earlier. He reenacted a debate from "Morning Joe" and offered holistic remedies for hyperhidrosis from "Dr. Oz." But once the food came—and Michael had a mouth full of spicy octopus—Bruce used the moment of silence to change the subject.

"So, have you given any thought to what we talked about?" Bruce asked. "You know, the 'us' stuff?"

Michael chewed more slowly in order to buy time.

"I know it freaks you out," Bruce continued. "It freaks me out too. It scares the shit out of me, actually. But I know I like you. You're my best friend. And when we get together...you know, like 'get together,' it's good. So I'm like, what are we waiting for?"

Michael finished chewing and swallowed his food. He wiped some spicy mayonnaise from his lips.

"Can I ask you something, though?" Michael said.

Bruce nodded.

"Why do you want something different from what we already have? Why do you want it to be so official? That doesn't even seem like you."

"Because…" Bruce said with his voice raised. Then he took a breath. "Because…" he continued, more softly, "…for me, more and more, I look at my life and I just want it to start moving in some kind of direction. I've given it a lot of thought and I don't really want to spend my whole life like I've been doing. It's not just about hook-ups for me anymore. I don't know why I'm feeling this way now. Maybe it's the shit with my mom. But I just have this feeling that I want something more, something with someone. And—O.K., here's the corny part—it would be cool if that someone was you. Like I said, you're my best friend."

Bruce stopped talking, looked away, and took a long sip of water. Michael remained quiet. His last conversation like this had been with Jimmy and that had turned out disastrously. But this was different. For one, he knew there'd be no big surprises with Bruce. Michael knew Bruce through and through, what he liked about him and what got on his nerves. On the one hand, this was comforting. But on the other hand, it also made it harder for him to completely give in to the idea of being with him. A little bit of mystery definitely helped when it came to relationships. When you didn't already know everything about a person, you could see a relationship as a potentially transformative journey rather than some predictable stroll down a frequently traveled path.

But then maybe predictability wasn't such a bad thing, especially given recent events. There were so many things that he knew for sure about Bruce, good things. He knew that Bruce would always have his back. Despite his many irritating faults, Bruce was solid.

Michael also knew that Bruce wanted many of the same things he himself wanted, like a feeling that his life was going somewhere. Michael knew that Bruce was offering a chance at happiness. Michael wondered: "How many chances does life give you to be happy? How many chances do you get to not be alone?"

"Maybe we should give it a shot," Michael said.

He looked up at Bruce. Michael had never seen his smile so brightly.

After dinner, they headed back to Bruce's place, high on hope. Bruce lifted Michael as they entered the living room, and they kissed for a long time with Bruce's hands cupped under Michael's ass. Slowly, Bruce moved them into the bedroom, then down onto the mattress.

"I want you to fuck me tonight," Bruce said.

"What? Really? I thought you never got fucked." Michael said, sitting up in the bed.

"Yeah. But tonight I think we should do something different, special."

"If you say so," said Michael.

They took off their clothes in a horny frenzy, with an assortment of socks, boxers, jeans, and shirts flying about the room. Michael grabbed a condom and a small tube of lube from a drawer on the nightstand. He put the condom on his already hard dick. Bruce was down on all fours at the edge of the bed.

"Dude, I seriously don't recommend 'doggy style' for your first anal," Michael said. "Why don't you ride me? That way you can control how deep it goes."

"Like you're that fucking big?" Bruce laughed.

"Fuck you," Michael said, falling back on the bed with his hard-on pointing toward the ceiling.

Bruce smiled, straddled Michael, and slowly worked his butt down on Michael's cock.

"Goddamn, you're tight!" Michael said. "Don't you ever finger yourself or, like, take a dump?"

"Shut the fuck up," Bruce said. "I'm trying to concentrate."

"Forget the KY," Michael continued. "Got any WD-40?"

Bruce playfully punched Michael in the chest. Then he closed his eyes and spread his ass cheeks with his hands.

Steadily, he worked himself further and further down Michael's cock until he was moving in a steady rhythm.

Michael asked, breathily, "You like it?"

Bruce sighed, in a bassy whisper, "Yeah. Fuck, yeah."

Hours later, after they'd both cum and fallen asleep together, Michael woke as if he'd heard an alarm. He was sweaty and could feel his pulse throb throughout his body. At first, he thought it might be food poisoning. All he wanted to do was drop to the floor, double over, and fold in on himself. But then he realized that the pain wasn't physical at all. What he felt was panic.

He knew, in that moment, without any doubt whatsoever, that he didn't want to be in a relationship with Bruce. He didn't have those feelings for him. He loved Bruce as a friend and enjoyed the occasional hook-ups. But that was it. It was instantly so clear. Why hadn't he come to this realization earlier? What the fuck was he going to do now?

Michael stayed in bed, thinking about all of this for about an hour. He'd close his eyes, open them, and then glance at the digital clock on the dresser. He didn't know whether he wanted the numbers to change faster or more slowly.

Around 6:00 a.m., he decided to get out of bed, taking care to gently remove Bruce's arm from around him and to ease off the mattress so that he didn't wake Bruce. Michael walked to the bathroom to take a piss, then he sat on the couch in the dark living room.

Bruce came in the room about an hour later, all sleepy-eyed and smiles.

"What are you doing out here?" Bruce asked. "Come back to bed."

"I'm not feeling well," Michael said.

"You're sick?"

"Not like that."

"Then what's up?"

"I don't know. Or, I mean, I do. But…"

"What are you talking about?"

"I think I fucked up."

"What do you mean?" Bruce asked, rubbing his eyes.

"I think I fucked up. About us."

"You're having second thoughts."

"I'm just not sure if this is right, us being together. I'm not sure if it's the right thing."

"Well, it was the right fucking thing earlier," said Bruce, his anger snapping him awake.

"Because I wanted it to be the right thing. Because I knew you wanted it. But the more I think about it...And, it's not just what I think, it's how I feel, deep down. I just feel that it's not right, like this is not what we're meant to be."

"Un-fucking-believable!" Bruce said.

"Just think about it. I mean, how do you know that this is what you really want, that I'm who you really want? How do you know that it's not just about the idea of being with someone?"

"Fuck you," Bruce said. "Seriously, fuck you. I'm so sick of your shit. What makes you think you know what I want?"

"I don't. I'm just asking the question. How do you know this is what you want? I mean, I don't know."

"Then speak for your fucking self. Just say that you don't know."

"O.K., I don't know."

"That's right," Bruce said. "And you'll never fucking know. That's your problem. You never fucking know what you want. And you know what? You're gonna end up with nothing, nothing and no one. You're gonna end up pathetic and alone. And it's gonna be because you never had the guts to stick with something."

"It's just that I don't want—"

"Go ahead and fucking say it. You just don't want me."

Chapter 23

Ziggy stood in the long line outside of the Mirror Ball, trying to act sober. He'd been drinking since...Well, he couldn't really remember when he hadn't been drinking. He was finding that vodka was compatible with a surprising number of beverages: Mountain Dew, Formula 50 Vitamin Water, and his friend Shereé's Organic Weightless Cranberry Tea. Shereé, a short, round girl who styled herself after Divine, the legendary drag queen from all those John Waters' movies, stood next to Ziggy in line.

Ziggy first met her at a party, where a skinny effete boy snootily accused her of being a cliché "fat fag hag." Shereé responded by grabbing the guy's nuts and shouting, "I am not a fag hag. I am a radical, dick-loving queer girl who will rip your balls off and chew them like Hubba Bubba." Ziggy had loved her ever since.

"Dude, stand up straight or they're not gonna let us in," Shereé said to Ziggy, who was getting wobbly.

"I'm good," Ziggy said. He grabbed her around the waist and pressed his face to hers.

"Keep telling yourself that," she said.

The truth was that Ziggy was far from good. He'd stopped going to classes and spent most of his days in bed. At night, he'd wander the city and hook up with guys on Scruff. He did anything to not think about the mistake that brought him to life.

The Mirror Ball line started to move and soon Ziggy and Shereé were nearing the doorman, a thick ex-military guy. He scrutinized Shereé license. Shereé barely looked 17, much less 21. But he nodded her in anyway.

Ziggy started to hand the doorman his ID, but he dropped it and almost fell on his face as he picked it up. Then he belched loudly upon returning upright. Shereé drew a tense breath. But the doorman waved them through.

"That was lucky," Shereé said, once inside.

"Lucky?" Ziggy said. "That guy fucked me, like, twice last week."

"Slut," Shereé said, shaking her head.

She grabbed Ziggy's arm and directed him toward the second floor balcony where they could look down on the dance floor. Ziggy felt woozy amidst the loud music and flashing lights.

"Oh shit," said Shereé, jolting Ziggy from his haze. "There's Andy, that straight shot boy I like. I'm gonna say hi."

Ziggy thought about stopping her. He'd learned firsthand that Andy was either gay or the world's best straight blowjob-giver. But he didn't have to energy to reach out his arm to her. Besides, he thought, people have to make their own fucking beds. How could he stop someone from making mistakes when he kept making so many of his own.

As he was immersed in his drunken thoughts, Ziggy felt a tap on his shoulder. At first he wasn't sure if it was happening in his head or actually occurring. Then he felt the tap again and turned around.

"You're Ziggy, right?" said a short nerdy guy with dark curly hair and thick-framed glasses.

"Who the fuck are you?"

"Arthur," he said, "you know like the king or the aardvark."

"What do you want, Arthur?" Ziggy said.

"I just wanted to introduce myself. I go to RISD too and we have a lot of mutual Facebook friends. Your name is always coming up as a 'People You Might Know.' So, I was like, let me introduce myself so that you are an actual person I do know."

A wave of drunken horniness came over Ziggy.

"Wanna suck my dick, Arthur?"

"Sure. I mean, yeah."

Even in the dark lighting, Ziggy could see Arthur's skin getting flushed.

"Let's go to the bathroom?" Ziggy directed.

"Oh no, I'm good," Arthur said.

A moment passed before Arthur's face registered that he'd misunderstood Ziggy's offer. "Oh, you mean to suck your dick? Here? In the bathroom? Now? No, I don't want to suck your dick now. Well, I mean, I do. But not here. But not really now either. I mean, I'd like to think that one day I could suck your dick. Like, I'd like to be in the queue for sucking your dick. I've thought about it. Even had a dream about it once although that's probably too much information—"

"Go the fuck away, Arthur."

"Sure. Sorry to bother you. But, um, nice to meet you anyway." Arthur started to walk away, but turned back around. "And you know all that stuff I said about your dick, about dreaming about it and all, I was just fucking around, trying to break the ice. I'm not, like, obsessed with your dick or anything. Seriously, your dick is safe with me." Arthur's face again turned a bruised red. "I mean, *from* me. Your dick is safe *from* me."

Ziggy turned his back to Arthur.

"O.K., then. Bye," Arthur said, walking away.

Ziggy wasn't sure why he'd been so mean to the guy. He just wasn't in the mood to be nice to anyone. Actually, he was in the mood to...

Moments later, Ziggy was standing on the wooden railing of the second floor balcony. His whole body seemed to wake up. All of the eyes in the place turned toward him. It was almost as if their collective gazes became a beam of light. Ziggy felt warm in the glow of it. He positioned his feet one in front of the other on the wooden railing. He let one foot slip over the side of the rail toward the dance floor. Then amidst an increasing roar of noise and people rushing toward him, he closed his eyes and hopped into the air.

Soon, he felt something that he'd never experienced before. He felt himself break.

Part Eight

Chapter 24

Michael lay on his bed with his face pressed on the pillow. He hoped that if he pushed his head deep enough into the pillow, he could force himself to sleep. He just wanted the day to end.

For the past few weeks, it seemed like there were too many hours in each day. He was finding it nearly impossible to fill them. He doubted that Bruce would ever speak to him again, and he really couldn't blame him. Ziggy, who had been such a big part of his life, was now removed from it. And Sidney was preoccupied with his new boyfriend. Michael was happy for Sidney. After all, Sidney hadn't had a real boyfriend in all the years that Michael had known him. Nevertheless, whenever he thought about Sidney's relationship, he couldn't help thinking about his lack of one.

Here he was, getting closer to 40 with every minute, yet he had no boyfriend and no prospects. He knew he'd done the right thing by breaking things off with Bruce. But that didn't mean he wanted to be alone forever.

Truth be told, there was only one person who Michael ever thought he could be with over the long haul. That was Chase. A part of him just felt that they would eventually be together. But with each day that possibility seemed more and more like a dream.

Michael rubbed his eyes a few times and stepped out of bed. He glanced at the clock on the DVR. He couldn't believe it was only 11:35 p.m. He walked into the bathroom, opened his medicine drawer, and got out an Ambien. It was the closest thing to a time eraser that he knew of. He was about to pop it in his mouth, when he heard his phone go off in the other room. It played a snippet from the Notorious B.I.G.'s "Warning." He hadn't heard that sound in a while. It was Ziggy's ringtone.

Michael arrived at the Rhode Island Hospital's emergency room with his heart thumping like a nightclub speaker. He'd felt like this ever since getting the call from Ziggy's phone. Ziggy wasn't on the line. It was one of Ziggy's friends telling him that there had been an accident at the Mirror Ball and Ziggy was in the hospital.

"I'll be right there," Michael said.

Michael parked his car and ran to the Emergency Room entrance. Standing outside the doors, under a silver awning, was a short guy with dark curly hair and glasses.

"Are you the, um, Ziggy's dad?" the guy asked.

The question startled Michael for a moment.

"Yeah. Yeah, I am," Michael said. "How is he?"

"They just took him down for one of those brain scan things. You know, where they slide you into a metal tube like on TV."

"An MRI?"

"Yeah, they're doing one of those."

"What the hell happened?" Michael asked.

"Not 100% sure. For some reason, he jumped up on the 2nd floor railing at Mirror Ball. And I guess he lost his balance and fell. He looked pretty busted up."

Michael was quiet, processing the story.

"I'm Arthur, by the way," said the guy, who offered his hand to Michael. Michael shook it firmly.

"You're a friend of Ziggy's?" Michael asked.

"Well, kinda sorta. We just officially met tonight. I go to RISD too and, you know, we have a lot of common Facebook friends. I mean, he's been coming up as a "Person You Might Know" on my homepage forever. But anyway, I'd been talking to him at the club tonight. And then when I saw him fall, I went over and kinda sat with him. One of his friends, some girl that he came with, couldn't stay because she was really drunk and had to hurl. Anyway, I was holding his hand, you know, the one that didn't look broken, and when the paramedics came, I guess they thought we were together. They asked if I wanted to ride with him to the hospital. I looked at Ziggy and was like, 'Do you want me to?' And he nodded yes. So here I am."

"Well, thanks for that." Michael said. "And Ziggy asked you to call me?"

"Yeah, well, the paramedics were asking who they should notify, and he told me to call you. He said you were his dad, but that it was a long story and weird. He didn't want his mom to know. So he gave me your name and I found it in his phone."

"Well, I better go inside and see what's going on."

"O.K.," Arthur said. "I think I might get going. It's probably gonna be a while before he wants to talk to anybody."

"O.K.," said Michael, shaking Arthur's hand again.

Arthur started to walk away, but stopped just before Michael stepped through the Emergency Room doors.

"But would you tell him I was here?" Arthur said. "He was really out of it so he might not even remember, but I'd kinda like him to know."

"Sure thing," said Michael.

Michael went into the hospital and got briefed by the attending physician, a short Arab woman. She told him that Ziggy was pretty busted up, breaking his left arm and hand, bruising his ribs and spraining his shoulder. But she didn't think there was anything wrong with his head, other than the fact that he lacked the good sense not to jump on a second floor railing.

"Kids these days," Michael said. He thought it sounded like something a dad would say.

The doctor gave him a look as if to say, "Really?" Then she walked away.

A few minutes later, a nurse led Michael behind a lime green curtain to see Ziggy, who was lying in the bed with his eyes closed. Michael walked over and gave Ziggy a visual once-over. His left arm and hand were bandaged and his face had some scratches on it. But other than that, he seemed fine. Michael began to go sit in the chair next to the bed when Ziggy opened his eyes.

"Hey," Ziggy said. Michael could tell from the look in Ziggy's eyes that he was more than a little dazed from the pain meds, not to mention whatever he drank or ingested before the fall.

"How do you feel?" Michael asked.

"Fucked," Ziggy said, hazily.

Michael started to ask, "What happened?" but stopped himself. "The doctor says you're gonna be fine."

"How did you know I was here?" Ziggy asked.

"Your friend called me."

"Shereé?"

"No, a guy."

Ziggy showed no sign of recognition.

"A guy named Arthur." Michael continued. "He said you told him to call me."

"I don't know," Ziggy said. "I don't really remember. Does my mom know? Don't tell her."

"I think you're gonna have to tell her." Michael said.

"She's gonna fucking freak."

"Yeah, but she has to know."

Ziggy didn't respond.

"I can call her for you if you want," Michael said.

"You don't mind?"

Michael shook his head.

"I've really been a dick to you." Ziggy said.

"No worries," said Michael.

Michael walked to the lobby to call Traci, who was understandably hysterical. Michael assured her that Ziggy was pretty much fine.

Once they finished talking, Michael walked back to Ziggy's bed and saw that he was asleep again. Michael sat in the chair next to the bed and reflected on the strangeness of the night, how he had started the evening feeling so disconnected from everything and everyone and now he was sitting at the bedside of his own flesh and blood.

Michael stayed in the chair for several more minutes, staring idly at the textured paneling of the wall behind the bed. Then Ziggy said something that startled him: "You're still here—

"

Michael sat up in the seat, rubbed his eyes. "Uh, yeah. You fell asleep. But I was just about to go. I talked to your mom and she'll be here first thing in the morning, so I'll—"

"No," said Ziggy. "I didn't mean it like that. I just...I was just noticing that you're still here."

"Yeah," said Michael. "I guess I am."

"Cool," Ziggy said, before closing his eyes again.

Chapter 25

About a week later, Michael walked especially slowly

on his way to the Mirror Ball. It was the kind of night where he

really wanted to take in the city, to let his eyes savor the beauty

of the old brick facades, uneven cobblestone streets, and bug-

eyed streetlights. Something about the city's solid, aged beauty

made him feel stronger. At one time, he thought he loved the city

because of Chase. Now, he realized that he loved the city

because it helped him survive losing Chase.

Michael turned onto Richmond St. and saw that there

was a short line snaking from the entrance to the club. He did a

quick scan of the line to see if he recognized anyone. He was relieved when he didn't see Bruce. He'd been avoiding the club for weeks because he hadn't wanted to run into Bruce. But tonight, Sidney had convinced him to come out. Sidney wanted Michael to get to know his new boyfriend. Michael didn't really want to spend an evening as the awkward appendage to a dewy-eyed new couple, but he was also tired of staying at home.

The line moved quickly and soon Michael was inside the club. RuPaul's "Supermodel (You Better Work)" played over the speakers.

"I thought you hated Retro Night," Michael said to Sidney when he found him standing by himself near the second floor bar.

"Yeah, well, Dante wanted to go out" Sidney said, giving Michael a hug.

Michael smiled and made a whip-cracking sound.

"Fuck off," Sidney said. "Relationships, especially new ones, make you do things that you wouldn't otherwise do."

"That's what sucks about them," Michael said.

"In a way, yes," Sidney said. "But in another way, it's good. It forces you out of yourself, makes you realize how stuck you'd been."

"You were stuck?"

"Of course, I was stuck," Sidney said, taking a sip from his Old Fashioned. "We all are. We all get caught in some idea of who we are, what our life is, how life is gonna be. It's easy to give up on the idea that life can still surprise us, surprise us in a good way."

Michael started to respond to Sidney, but they were interrupted by a tall, brown-skinned guy who Sidney introduced as Dante. Michael had the vague notion that he had seen him somewhere before, but he couldn't quite place it. Michael noticed the relaxed, intimate way that Dante kept touching Sidney and sort of leaned his butt against Sidney's knee.

They talked for a few more minutes before Michael excused himself to go to the restroom. Once again Michael opened the door to the second floor bathroom and was struck by the thick, acidy smell of fresh puke. This was becoming a common occurrence. Holding his breath, he backed out of the doorway and headed to the third-floor bathroom. He pushed the door open to the stairwell, stepped inside, and ran straight into Bruce.

He looked at Bruce's face and saw anger rise in his eyes. Bruce's forehead clenched tightly. Suddenly, Bruce stretched out his arms, grabbed Michael, and then slammed him against the wall of the stairwell. Michael fell to the floor.

"What the fuck?" Michael yelled, pulling himself up.

Bruce stepped back, shook his body out like a fighter in the ring.

"I've been thinkin' about doing that for a long fucking time," Bruce said.

"You've been thinking about slamming me against a wall?" Michael said. He rubbed the back of his head.

"No, generally what I thought was a lot worse. You know, punching your face in, ripping off your balls…"

"You're a fucking lunatic!"

"I was really pissed off. But I think I got it out of my system. No, wait a minute…"

Bruce took a playful swing at Michael's head. Michael ducked, and Bruce started laughing hysterically.

"You're an asshole." Michael said.

Bruce reached out for Michael and said, "O.K., let's get this over with."

"What in the holy fuck are you talking about?" Michael asked.

"Let's 'hug it out.' I'm tired of this weirdness, all this bullshit. Let's just end it."

"You're not still mad?"

"Do you really think I'm gonna let a narcissistic twit like you turn me into some scorned little bitch?"

Michael felt both deeply insulted and like he'd been bestowed with a coarse form of grace.

"Come on, let's go upstairs and have a drink." Bruce said.

"Why should I go upstairs with someone who just attacked me?"

"'Cause I'm askin' you to," Bruce said

"Do I need security?"

"No, I got that out of my system," Bruce laughed. "So, will you have a drink with me?"

"Begrudgingly," Michael said, before following Bruce upstairs.

They walked over to an empty part of the bar and sat down. Bruce ordered drinks for both of them.

"So, how have you been?" Bruce asked, taking the first sip from his beer.

"Well, other than the possible concussion you gave me…"

Bruce shrugged.

"I've been…," Michael said. "It's been a rough couple of months. But you know, here I am and shit."

"I've missed you," Bruce said. "I really have."

"I've missed you too," Michael said. "That was, like, the whole point. I didn't want to fuck up our friendship."

"Yeah," Bruce said. "I'm sorry everything got screwed up. I just…I just had all these feelings. I mean, I know there's a connection between us. That's why I thought we were supposed to be more than friends. And now, I don't know. Sometimes I think maybe we are; other times, I think maybe not."

Michael took a sip from his drink.

"You know what happened that day you left my house?" Bruce said.

"You mean the day you told me to 'get the fuck out?'"

"Yeah."

"I got the fuck out."

"No, what happened to me, dick hole?"

"What?"

"Later that day, I couldn't find my mom. I realized that I hadn't heard from her in a while, so I went up to her part of the house and she was nowhere to be found. I called her cell phone, but it was on the dresser, plugged in."

"What did you do?"

"I didn't panic at first. Sometimes she wanders around the neighborhood and shit. I got in my truck and drove around, but I didn't see her anywhere. That's when I started to get scared. I didn't know where to look. I was about to go door-to-door when I got this call. It was from this guy who manages

Iggy's Doughboys and Chowder House in Warwick. She used to go there a lot with my dad before they moved to Florida."

Bruce took another sip from his beer and then continued: "Apparently, she had taken a cab there, eaten a lobster roll, and was just sitting around for a couple of hours. She told the manager she was waiting for someone. But, you know, after a while, he realized that something wasn't right. He started talking to her and figured out she was lost. Long story short. She had my number on an emergency contact card in her wallet. Thank God, she had that with her."

"Yeah," Michael said.

"So, I'm rushing over to the restaurant, and the whole time, I'm thinking that my mom is confused about so many things and has lost so many memories, but she still remembered this place where she used to eat with my dad. She still remembered loving someone and what she used to do with the person she loved. And I just wondered, really fucking wondered, if someone will ever love me that deep, you know? Will I ever mean that much to someone? That's all I've been thinking about lately."

"Join the club," said Michael.

"I thought for a while that you and me could have something like that. That's what I wanted. But I've learned…at least, I think I've learned…I'm *trying* to learn that you can't force that shit."

"How's your mom now?"

"Fine. I mean, the same."

Bruce finished his beer and then stood up abruptly. "This is getting way too depressing. Let's go back downstairs. I need to find something to dip my dick in tonight."

Michael laughed, truly relaxing for the first time that night.

On the second floor landing, Michael and Bruce surveyed the dancefloor below. Michael spotted Jimmy dancing with his boyfriend. Once again, Michael felt good about being able to look at the two of them without feeling jealousy or that sense that he might have missed out on something.

Michael felt good about his choice not to move in with Jimmy at that stage in their relationship, just as he felt secure in his decision to break things off romantically with Bruce. Neither situation had felt right, not in the way that he believed true love should feel, or how he wanted it to feel. He sensed that if he had forced himself to go through with either situation, he would have one day regretted not holding out for true love. Sometimes Michael wondered if, for him, the greatest love of all was the romance of possibility.

#

The next morning, Michael sat across from Ziggy at a table at Brickway on Wickenden. Their waitress had just set down their omelettes, two Eau Claries. They bumped hands reaching for the pepper at the same time.

"I'll rock-paper-scissors you for it," said Ziggy.

"You go ahead since you only have one good arm."

Ziggy laughed and lifted up his cast. "Yeah, good thing it was my left hand or else I'd be having some serious fapping issues."

Michael laughed and looked around the room. His last time here was with Traci. He'd been so pissed. He couldn't even remember if he'd finished his food.

"How's your mom?" Michael asked. He took a bite of his omelette.

"She's good," Ziggy said. "Less worried now that I'm healing and not drinking as much."

"But you are still drinking?"

"Not much. You know, just to party and get buzzed. Not to, you know, kill myself."

"It's good that you have a sense of humor about it."

"What's my choice? The whole year has been like a fucking joke. I'd be laughing my nuts off if it hadn't happened to me."

"And how's school?"

"It's cool. You know, final projects and shit…"

"Wait a minute," Michael interrupted. "I'm sorry."

"For what?" Ziggy said. He looked up from his food.

"I'm asking you a million fucking questions."

"It's O.K.," Ziggy said.

"No, but I sound like your…I don't know. I don't want it to be like that."

"How do you want it to be?"

"That's the fucked up thing," Michael said. "I don't know how it should be. Like how are we supposed to act?"

"Yeah, I don't want you patting me on the head, calling me 'Sonny Boy' and shit."

They both laughed.

"But, seriously," Michael said, "I would like to figure something out. I hope that we can be something, whatever that is. It just has to work for us."

"What's the first step?" Ziggy asked.

"I guess this is," said Michael.

Michael and Ziggy finished eating. Michael paid the bill and they walked out to the street. Michael was surprised to see Arthur, Ziggy's friend from the hospital, standing outside.

"Oh, hi," Arthur said to both of them. "I'm early."

"You're always early," said Ziggy, pulling Arthur into a hug and giving him a kiss on the top of his head.

Arthur broke away, blushing. He offered his hand to Michael and said, "Good to meet you again, sir, under, well, circumstances that don't require critical care."

"Yeah, it's good seeing you again too," Michael said. "But you don't have to call me 'sir.' Actually, please don't."

"Sorry. I was just trying to be polite, since you're, like, Ziggy's dad and all."

Michael was quiet. The whole "dad" thing still made him uncomfortable. Arthur continued: "Um, and you should know that I have nothing but the most honorable intentions toward your son."

Ziggy stifled a laugh.

"It's cool, "Michael said.

Arthur went on, "And, you know, if there ever comes a time when I'd want to gay-marry him, I will certainly ask you for his hand in advance."

"O.K., lil' dude, you're taking it way too far again," said Ziggy, pulling Arthur into another hug.

"Sorry," Arthur said, and then turned to Michael, "I just really like him."

Michael smiled. He felt a strange sensation rise within him. Was it pride?

Michael gave a hug to both Ziggy and Arthur, before heading down Wickenden to walk home. He got about a half block away, when he felt compelled to look back. He stopped for a moment and watched Ziggy and Arthur walk slow and close in the other direction. Then Ziggy turned around and saw Michael looking at him. Ziggy smirked, shook his head, and gave Michael the finger.

About the Author

Craig Seymour is a writer whose work has been published in *The Washington Post*, *Entertainment Weekly*, and *Vibe*, among other publications. He has taught writing at the University of Massachusetts at Dartmouth and Northern Illinois University. He holds a Ph.D. in American Studies from the University of Maryland at College Park, and is the author of two other books: *Luther: The Life & Longing of Luther Vandross* (HarperCollins, 2004) and *All I Could Bare: My Life in the Strip Clubs of Gay Washington, D.C.* (Simon & Schuster, 2008).

As a bonus, get the audio version of his memoir *All I Could Bare for* free: http://vibedeck.com/craigseymour/107709

craigseymour.com

@craigspoplife

craigspoplife@gmail.com

Made in the USA
Las Vegas, NV
23 November 2020